Nature Girl

jane Kelley

Random House New York

*The author is extremely grateful for the wisdom
and support of her agent, Linda Pratt,
and her editor, Shana Corey.*

Text copyright © 2010 by Jane Kelley
Illustrations copyright © 2010 by Heather Palisi

All rights reserved. Published in the United States by Random House Children's
Books, a division of Random House, Inc., New York.

Random House and the colophon are registered trademarks of Random House, Inc.

Visit us on the Web! www.randomhouse.com/kids

Educators and librarians, for a variety of teaching tools, visit us at
www.randomhouse.com/teachers

Library of Congress Cataloging-in-Publication Data
Kelley, Jane A.
Nature Girl / by Jane Kelley. — 1st ed.
p. cm.
Summary: While spending the summer in Vermont, eleven-year-old Megan gets lost on
the Appalachian Trail and she decides to hike to Massachusetts to visit her best friend.
ISBN 978-0-375-85634-1 (trade) — ISBN 978-0-375-95634-8 (lib. bdg.) —
ISBN 978-0-375-85635-8 (trade pbk.) — ISBN 978-0-375-89326-1 (e-book)
[1. Survival—Fiction. 2. Lost children—Fiction. 3. Self-confidence—Fiction.
4. Friendship—Fiction. 5. Best friends—Fiction. 6. Appalachian Trail—Fiction.
7. Vermont—Fiction.] I. Title.
PZ7.28168Nd 2010
[Fic]—dc22
2009019078

Printed in the United States of America
10 9 8 7 6 5 4 3 2 1

First Edition

For Sofia, my very first reader.
And especially for Lee, who always believed in me.

CONTENTS

It's not the mountain we conquer, but ourselves.
—Sir Edmund Hillary, who climbed Mount Everest

Nature Girl

1
The Hundred-Year-Old Maple

"Can you hear me now?"

I creep a little further out along the tree branch.

"Lucy, are you there?"

I hear a little mumbling. I switch hands so that the cell phone is pressed against my right ear, six inches closer to my best friend.

"Lucy, you've just got to be there!"

My parents said the cell phone could only be used for emergencies. But this IS an emergency! My miserableness has swelled to monstrous proportions like the Barney balloon in the Macy's Thanksgiving Day Parade. Besides, since I'm hiding in a tree, my parents won't even know I called Lucy until months from now when they get the phone bill. Then I won't care how they punish me because I'll be back home in New York City, far, far away from Nowheresville, Vermont.

"LUCY!"

I shouldn't have yelled. I quickly look around to see if anyone heard me. But no one's paying any attention to me—as usual. Mom is on the other side of the farmhouse, painting the barn. I don't mean really painting it (even though it sure could use a new coat of red). No, she's making a painting of it. "Trying to capture the essence of its heroism as it stands against the march of time." I'm not kidding you. Mom actually said that. Dad is at the far side of the field, sketching the tumbledown pile of rocks at the edge of the Woods. Anywhere else in the world, people would immediately get rid of that useless safety hazard. But up here, everybody worships that rock pile because it's an authentic Vermont stone wall.

My sister, Ginia, is inside the farmhouse. Her name is really VIRginia, but ever since she turned sixteen, she has a fit if you call her that. She's really good at drawing. She can draw just about anything—even galloping horses. But she's probably doing another self-portrait so her squinty little eyes can be big and beautiful. She gets to spend hours mooning into a mirror and playing with her hair because my parents think that's *ART*.

I'm supposed to be doing *ART* too. Every morning, the time between nine o'clock and noon is dedicated to "creative pursuits." That's my parents' idea of a fun summer. Can you believe it? Three whole hours—every day? I told them that I couldn't do anything for three whole hours—not even things I liked. Dad just smiled and repeated one of his annoying sayings, "Practice makes perfect."

But he was lying. Practice won't help my painting or drawing or anything else.

The trouble is, I don't have any important talents. That became really obvious last fall when I started middle school. The first thing that happened was all the sixth graders had to demonstrate how great they were at singing and dancing and painting and showing off. Then the talent teachers chose kids for their workshops. I was hoping I could be in the chorus with Lucy. But I didn't get picked for that. I didn't even get picked for drawing. In fact, I guess you could say I didn't get picked for anything. I got put in photography with all the other kids they didn't know what to do with. I mean, anyone can point a camera at something and push a button. Unfortunately they didn't have a workshop for doodling and hanging out with your best friend. Because those are the only things I'm any good at.

Maybe you think that doodling is drawing. They both use paper and pencil, right? I kind of thought that too. So on the first morning of *ART* time, I sketched myself standing next to the farmhouse. I can't draw people, but you could recognize me by my frizzy hair. Then I made a swarm of mosquitoes attacking me. Only I didn't actually draw them because they're too tiny and complicated; I just covered the page in dots. Unfortunately Mom walked past while I was stabbing the paper with

3

my pen. I tried to keep her from seeing what I was doing, but she looked anyway. She opened her mouth like she wanted to say something. Then she shut it again. Then she sighed. So I crumpled up the paper and threw it away.

And that's the difference. Drawing ends up in museums. Doodling ends up in the trash.

Every day after that, I just wrote words like art and Vermont in my sketchbook and completely scribbled them out. Mom complained that I wasn't creating; I was destroying. So I told her what Dad always says. *ART* is all about personal expression. And ripping the page with my pencil sure expressed my person.

Summer vacation should NOT be like this. If I had

known what my parents were going to do to me, I would've gotten such bad grades that they would have had to send me to summer school instead. But this is our first summer up here. I had never even been to Vermont.

Besides, Lucy was supposed to be with me. Lucy has been my best friend since she taught me how to whistle in preschool. That's almost two-thirds of our entire lives. If she had come, every bad thing would have been bearable. No cable TV? No Internet? Mice poop in the cupboards? A million bloodsucking insects? Who cares? Whatever happens, we roll our eyes and laugh about it. Because that's what friends do.

Only Lucy couldn't come. Her mom, Alison, has Hodgkin's lymphoma. Don't bother asking who Hodgkin is. No one will tell you. They'll just get mad at you for making jokes, when you really want to know. All they would say was that it was a *good* kind of cancer. And everybody was glad about that.

So then I thought, Well, okay, maybe Lucy won't come for the WHOLE summer. Maybe we won't have the endless sleepover we planned. Maybe we'll just be together for five or four or three weeks. But at the very last minute, Lucy told me she wasn't coming to Vermont AT ALL.

She and her mom are spending the summer with her grandmother. Mrs. T. has a summerhouse in Massachusetts, just about an hour's drive from us in Vermont. So Lucy isn't that far away. She could have come for a week or a day—or five minutes.

Or I could have gone down there. Lucy and Alison were always planning to climb this mountain that's practically in Mrs. T.'s backyard. Mount Greylock is really cool. It has a stone tower and a souvenir stand where you can get ice cream after you make it to the top. Now that's my kind of mountain. So I said to Lucy, maybe I could come for a short visit and my dad could drive us all up there—even Alison. I thought that was a terrific idea. Only Lucy said her mom has a different mountain to climb this summer. And it isn't the kind of mountain I can climb—even if I want to.

So here I am. Stuck in Nowheresville, Vermont, without my best friend, being tortured by my family. I know you think I'm exaggerating but I'm not! This is what happened.

Yesterday Mom made me go swimming for exercise. Only there aren't any swimming pools up here. Oh no. Why would we want a clean cement bottom when there could be yucky gunk? We went to a big hole in the ground filled with mud. On top of the mud there's maybe ten inches of water. On top of the water is a layer of floating green scum. And Mom expected me to swim in that!

There were lots of other kids and teenagers there—including Ginia's new boyfriend, Sam, who lives up here ALL YEAR ROUND. They all jumped right in, like they didn't know how gross that pond water was. Like maybe they had never seen an actual swimming pool. I sat on a rock as far away from the scum as I could get.

Sam and these boys started teasing me. Why wasn't I swimming? Didn't I know how to swim? I told them, of course I did. Only I wouldn't swim in that scummy cesspool. So they threw me in the water.

Did Ginia save me? No. She laughed! Later, when I told Mom and Dad, Mom said it was a good thing. And Dad said someday I would look back on it and be grateful. GRATEFUL? That I was totally slimed by those jerks and humiliated forever?

Since my family had NO sympathy for me, I begged them to let me call Lucy.

But they wouldn't because the cell phone is just for emergencies. Unless it's the weekend, when there are free minutes. I was supposed to wait until Saturday! Then Mom suggested I write Lucy a letter. What century does she think this is? What's the point of civilization if you can't call the only person in the whole world who truly cares about you?

This morning, my hair still smelled like gunk. I felt like I really would die if I didn't talk to Lucy. I waited until my family were all off doing their *ART.* I snuck out to the car. I made believe I was looking for a pencil I dropped. Then I carefully opened the glove compartment and took out the little silver phone.

I almost cried when I saw its shiny surface. You won't believe this, but practically everything else in Vermont is made of cloth or pottery or wood. I slid the phone into my pocket. I got out of the car and held up the pencil to

7

show anyone who was spying why I had gone over there. Then I casually walked across the yard to the maple tree.

Mom and Dad love that tree. Every morning at breakfast they say, "Isn't it wonderful that this syrup came from our very own Hundred-Year-Old Maple!" As if a little sticky sauce makes up for being deprived of every single thing I like to do.

The Hundred-Year-Old Maple has boards nailed into its trunk. Not by us—oh no, we love the tree—but by whatever kids lived here before. The boards go up about ten feet to a branch that sticks out horizontally. I grabbed hold of a board and climbed. The boards wobbled, but I made it to the horizontal branch. I carefully stood up, holding on to another branch with my left hand.

A brown bird was just a few feet above me. It cocked its head and gave me a look like, "What are you doing in my tree?" Believe me, I didn't want to be up there. But I had to get high enough so that the cell phone signal could make it over the mountains and out of Vermont.

As I punched the buttons with my right thumb, I worried that Alison would answer. I never knew how to talk to her anymore. You couldn't say, "Hi, how are you?" to a sick person.

Luckily Mrs. T. answered the phone. She usually loved to chat. But when I asked if she had seen any summer theater, she told me to call back later. Only I couldn't call later. I was already in the tree! So I told her I had to speak to Lucy. It was an emergency.

Then Lucy got on the phone and said, "What's wrong, Megan?"

Her voice sounded far away. When I said how good it was to talk to her, she didn't say anything. That was when I started shouting, "Lucy, are you there? Lucy, you've just got to be there! LUCY!"

Lucy isn't answering. Something is wrong with the cell phone. I need to find a spot with a better signal. I inch way out on the branch. The bird flies away. The further out I go, the more the branch sinks from my weight. But I can't worry about that now.

"LUCY!"

Finally she says, "Stop yelling, Megan. I can hear you. We're waiting for Mom's doctor to call. Mom's really nervous."

Lucy sounds nervous too, like she's having trouble breathing. I wonder if I should try to make her laugh. I love her laugh. It doesn't come from her mouth or her nose; it comes all the way from her belly—especially when she laughs at my jokes.

"Should I read you more of Ginia's diary? Remember? 'Oh how I love the hair on Sam's knuckles.'" To tell the truth, I made that up. Ginia doesn't even have a diary.

"Some other time, okay, Megan?"

"That's okay. I can't get it now anyway. I'm in a tree."

"What?"

"Don't worry. I haven't turned into a Nature Girl. I came up here to call you. You won't believe what happened to me yesterday. Mom took me to this pond to swim, but it was full of gunk and frog pee."

But she interrupts. "Grandma said you said it was an emergency."

"It IS an emergency."

"If it happened yesterday, it can't be an emergency today."

Lucy gets all picky about stuff like that. It can be very annoying. So I get a little mad because she isn't really listening to me. "It IS an emergency because I'm still suffering. You don't know how I'm suffering. Nobody does. Nobody cares."

"Nobody cares because you aren't really suffering!"

"My hair stinks like rotten leaves! I'll never get the slime out! Ever!"

"At least you HAVE hair!"

Lucy has hair too. Her hair is short and straight and shiny black. But Alison doesn't have hair right now.

There's a big silence again. Only this time I know it's not the phone.

"Please don't be mad at me, Lucy. I can't help saying stupid stuff because I really am suffering. You don't know because you aren't here. But you should be. You should have come to Vermont with me like you promised!"

10

I stamp my foot for emphasis. Then I hear a loud crack.

There's a moment when I think, Oh no, this can't be happening. But I'm wrong. It is happening.

The branch breaks and I fall smack to the ground.

I guess I scream; I don't know. I slam into the dirt so hard, the air is knocked out of my lungs. But it feels like more than that. It feels like my actual self whooshes out of my body and up into the sky. I hover over my old body. It looks really weird with its legs and arms sprawled in crazy angles on top of all these sticks and leaves. As I float higher and higher, I'm so happy that I'm finally getting away from Vermont.

Mom and Dad and Ginia run toward my body, carrying their paintbrushes.

"Megan, what happened?" Mom says.

"Looks like she fell," Dad says.

Mom drops her paintbrush and kneels beside me. She brushes the hair back from my face and strokes my forehead like she used to when I was little.

"Is she unconscious?" Dad kneels on my other side.

They both look at me with worried faces. The past few weeks, their eyes were narrow slits that zapped me with laser beams of anger. But now their eyes are sympathetic and wide. They gently pat me all over, feeling for broken bones. After I slip back into my body, I try to smile at them. I feel really horrible and yet somehow better than I've felt since we came to Vermont.

And then, out of the corner of my eye, I see Ginia pick up a small shiny rectangle.

I gasp.

"Did that hurt, honey?" Mom says.

"Maybe her leg is broken," Dad says.

I send all kinds of sister messages to Ginia. Like, I will give you my allowance for a year and never tease you about Sam again and be your personal slave if only you put that little insignificant silver thing into your pocket and keep your big mouth shut.

She smiles at me. I smile back. I'm so relieved. I love my sister.

The silver glints in the sun as she holds out her hand. "Look what I found. I wonder how our cell phone got way over here on the ground?"

From the phone, a little voice says, "Hello? Megan? What's happening?"

It's Mrs. T.

What happened to Lucy? She must be really mad at me. And that makes me mad. I jump up. "It isn't my fault. I had to call. It was an emergency! None of this would have happened if you let me call Lucy last night. But you only do what you want. You never do what I want." I stamp my foot.

"I guess her leg isn't broken." Dad walks over to the tree.

Mom sighs as she takes the phone from Ginia.

"Hello, Mrs. T.? Don't worry about Megan. She's fine. How's Alison?"

I'm not fine. I'm shaking. My head hurts, my arm is scraped, my legs are scratched, and my favorite black T-shirt with the New York subway map on it is ripped. But I'm not lucky enough to be taken to a hospital where a nice nurse will fluff up my pillows and I can lie around watching cable TV. I have no broken bones to heal.

Dad examines the tree limb. The part where it broke looks like a big angry mouth with jagged teeth. Dad lifts the branch. For a moment, the mouth is closed. But then he lets it fall down again and the mouth opens wider than ever.

"I'm sure the doctor will have good news. Please give Alison our love. Let us know if there's anything we can do. Good-bye." Mom hangs up the phone.

She doesn't even ask me if I want to say good-bye to Lucy. But I can't talk anyway; I'm trying so hard not to cry. I hate them. I hate them all. I limp toward the house.

I only get about three steps before I hear Mom say, "Where do you think you're going? We're not finished here, Megan Knotts."

Let this be a lesson for you. As bad as you think things are, they can always get worse.

2
Punishments

These are my punishments.

First: no using the cell phone for the rest of July. This is especially painful because now I can't call Lucy to find out if she's mad at me.

Second: reparations to the tree. Reparations are what Dad makes me do to try to fix things. I have to write a letter to the farmer we're renting the house from. I have to pay for a visit from the tree doctor with my own money. And I have to write an Apology Poem to the tree and actually go outside and read it to the tree. Out loud.

Oh tree, oh big fat leafy green tree
I'm really very sorry that I hurt thee!
oh tree, oh giver of oxygen to me,
Please accept my sincere apology.

Third (and most horrifying): no TV for the rest of the summer. None. Not the news, not the PBS station, not even that awful yoga tape *Kundalini Kids*. No screen time whatsoever no matter how educational or boring.

Mom says this isn't a punishment; it's a way of helping me. Of course, my mother is one of those anti-TV types. The only show she likes to watch is the summer Olympics and that only comes on once every four years.

"We know you've been unhappy up here, sweetheart. It isn't as much fun for you without Lucy. But you haven't given Vermont a fair chance."

"What's that supposed to mean?"

"Stop wishing for what you can't have. Live where you are. This is the country. You should embrace nature. Dive into that pond."

That's easy for her to say. She doesn't have slime growing in her hair. She wouldn't have noticed even if she did. Her hair is short and spiky. She likes to dye the gray parts different colors anyway. But my hair is light brown and would reach way past my shoulders if it weren't so curly. I already washed it six times, and let me tell you, that green is not going away.

"What does that disgusting pond have to do with watching TV?" I say.

"TV only provides a temporary diversion. It fills you with sweets so you can't have a healthy hunger for real pleasures that will truly nurture you."

I hate it when my mother rambles on like a crazy

15

person. I make the mistake of rolling my eyes. Then she gets mad and says the thing a kid can never argue with.

"It's for your own good."

She snatches the rabbit-ear antenna off the top of the TV and takes it upstairs. *Clomp, clomp, clomp.* The sound of her clogs on the wooden floor is like someone hammering nails into my coffin.

I'm stunned. I can't believe she took the antenna.

"Whatever happened to spanking? Can't you beat me and get it over with? Now I'll be in agony ALL SUMMER LONG!"

I fall to the floor and wail so loud the dog starts barking. Does Mom care? No. I could be oozing blood from an organ that burst when I fell out of the tree, but she doesn't even bother to check. She comes back downstairs, without the antenna, and picks up the dog to comfort HIM.

That's when I decide I won't suffer alone.

I plan out separate tortures for each of them.

Ginia gets the cut-ahead treatment. Whenever she's on her way to the bathroom (and oh by the way there is only ONE stinking bathroom in the place—unless you want to count the actual I-kid-you-not wooden outhouse by the barn), I run and duck in ahead of her. Then she yells, "Mom!" and I say, "Sorry, but I really have to go." Then I run the water in the sink like I'm peeing buckets and roar with silent laughter while she pounds on the door.

16

Dad's punishment is more devious. My parents are both high school art teachers. But Dad especially loves to tell you stuff. Sometimes he talks about something interesting, like how they made the original Disney cartoons. (Did you know they had to draw every little flapping wing over and over by hand, since they didn't have any computers?) But now whenever he tells one of his stories, I just stare at him. When he finishes, I say, "And I needed to know all that because?" Then he gets a hurt look and smooths his beard. (That's right—he grew a beard, because it's some kind of Vermont law that ALL men up here have to have furry faces.) Finally he says, "I guess I thought it was kind of interesting."

But the best punishment is for Mom.

I start spending all my time staring at the blank TV screen.

"What's wrong, Megan?" Mom asks.

I don't answer. I just sigh.

"Can't you find anything to do?"

I sigh again.

"Sitting there will only make you more depressed."

I shake my head. I'm already as depressed as anyone could be.

Then Mom starts in on her list of WHY-DON'T-YOUs. Why don't you read, why don't you draw, why don't you write Lucy a letter, why don't you walk the dog, why don't you do yoga, why don't you explore that hiking trail behind the field?

I still don't say anything. Not talking to her is part of her torture. I hear the anger rising in her voice like the water filling up the back of the toilet. Then SWOOSH— out comes a great flushing rush of rage. MEGAN, YOU CAN'T SPEND THE REST OF YOUR LIFE LIKE THIS!

Part of me thinks, Sure I can. But another part of me thinks, What if I have to?

This lasts for a whole week. Just between you and me, I'm getting pretty sick of it. The only good part is that whenever I stare at the blank TV, I pretend I'm watching home movies of my favorite days with Lucy.

We've had so many wonderful days together. There was the day Mrs. T. took us to see a Broadway show and we got to go backstage and meet the star and ride in three different taxis. There was the day that Lucy and I made an entire city out of shoe boxes and then we played like we were giants destroying everything. There was our first sleepover, when we pretended we were camping out in Lucy's living room and had s'mores and everything. There was the day that Alison took us to her office on the fifty-second floor and we got to meet an author who was very nice even though we never heard of the book she wrote.

But the most perfect day was one year ago, in the summer right after fifth grade. (To be honest, there aren't very many happy memories from sixth grade.) As a reward for surviving elementary school, Dad took Lucy and me to

Coney Island in Brooklyn. First we went to the aquarium. The penguins were cute and everything, but the best part was when I got Lucy laughing by pretending to kiss this big, fat, ugly walrus through the viewing window and calling him "my Blubber Boy." As we started to leave, the walrus followed me. That made Lucy laugh even more. Luckily the walruses are right by the bathroom, because she laughed so much she desperately had to go!

Then we went across the boardwalk to the beach. Lucy found two lucky quarters when we were making sand creatures. After I didn't find any no matter how deep a hole I dug, she said I should have the one with the state of Missouri on it because my name starts with M. Lucy always shares like that. We spent so much time making mythological beasts that Dad said we didn't have time for the amusement park. I started getting upset, but Lucy had the brilliant idea of asking Dad what his favorite ride was. He told a long story about taking Mom on the Wonder Wheel. Lucy said he just HAD to ride it again to keep the memory alive. And you know what? He agreed! But first we had corn dogs for dinner—hot dogs dipped in dough and cooked in a yummy way. Then we all rode the Wonder Wheel. (Luckily Dad sat alone in a car with just his memories.) From the top, we had the most incredible view of the ocean and Brooklyn and everything like it all belonged to us. I was so happy, I said, "Oh, Lucy, the sky is glowing pink from my happiness." But Lucy didn't say, "Duh, the sun is setting," like Ginia would have. Lucy sighed and said, "The world outside and the world inside match."

Oh, I really loved that day. I play it over and over again.

Then one morning, eight whole days after I spoke to Lucy and fell out of the tree, Mom and Dad are sitting side by side at the table when I come down for breakfast.

"Megan," Dad says. "We give up."

"You do?" I say.

Mom nods.

My stubbornness has worn them down. They've finally realized it's really strength. I try to be cool but my heart's jumping. HOORAY! HOORAY! Let's get this conversation over with so I can watch something on TV before *ART* time begins—I wouldn't even care if it was *Dora the Explorer*.

"This past week, we've waited for you to come to your senses," Dad says.

"To do something positive for a change," Mom says.

Actually I thought my torture plans were pretty positive.

"You're going to be twelve at the end of August. You should be able to make wise choices. But you haven't done that. So we have to make you do what's good for you," Dad says.

"It's our duty to assert our authority as your parents," Mom says.

My mood drops like a rock. Why didn't I pay more attention when we studied the American Revolution at school? If I can come up with a good quote about declaring my independence to pursue happiness, I have a chance. But unfortunately I spent the entire unit drawing macaroni noodles on Yankee Doodle's hat.

"You're wasting your summer," Dad says.

Whose fault is that? (I don't say.)

"You could be in danger of wasting your whole life," Mom says.

Look who's talking. (I don't say.)

"We have decided to start you on a plan of self-improvement," Dad says.

What else is new? (I don't say.)

"This morning you are going on a hike," Mom says.

I'm stunned. They're giving up *ART* time to punish me?

"With Ginia," Dad says.

"What?" Ginia runs into the kitchen. "But you said Sam and I could go."

"You can go," Mom says. "And you can take Megan."

Ginia turns a weird kind of reddish purple and her eyes bug out. I put my hand over my face. A smirk is beginning to spread. If you have siblings, then you already know this—the next best thing to your own happiness is your sister's misery.

"But Sam was going to show me the beaver dam," Ginia says.

21

"I'm sure Megan would like to see it too," Dad says.

"You bet," I say enthusiastically.

Ginia's really squirming now. I know the only thing she wants Sam to show her is a place to M*A*K*E O*U*T.

"What about her injuries?" Ginia says.

She is totally desperate. But it doesn't work.

"Go put on sturdy shoes," Mom says.

When she says that, I start to worry. What kind of a hike is this going to be? Maybe I should have thought about it some more before I agreed to go.

As I climb the stairs, I'm thinking that maybe I won't be able to find my shoes. I hear Ginia trying to get Mom and Dad to change their minds. That's when I find out that their plan isn't just about improving me. Something's wrong with the air-conditioning in the car. Dad has to drive it halfway across Vermont to Rutland to get it fixed. Mom wants to go with him and visit some painter friends who are staying near there. But she doesn't want to leave me alone in the farmhouse. I run downstairs with the answer to everybody's problem.

"I can go with Mom and Dad to Rutland." Any city, even one in Vermont, is better than a hike.

"That's right," Ginia says.

"I'm sorry, Ginia. But I don't want you and Sam going off into the Woods by yourselves," Mom says.

"Why not? We're not going to DO anything," Ginia says.

"If you're not going to do anything, then there's no

22

reason why Megan can't go with you. She can spend the night with Sam's family too," Mom says.

So we're all doomed, except Mom and Dad. After *ART* time is over, they get to drive to Rutland, see a movie while they wait for the car to be fixed, and then spend the night with their friends, who probably have an Internet connection AND cable TV.

Mom goes upstairs to get my sneakers and my school backpack. It's still full of sixth-grade junk from last year. Notes from Lucy, unfinished homework assignments, my wallet with my emergency money, and a book that was supposed to be for independent reading. *My Side of the Mountain.* It's about a boy who runs away and lives by himself on a mountain. Dad gave it to me last Christmas. It's the kind of book grown-ups think you should read just because they liked it when they were kids in the last century. Dad wrote on the inside flap, "For Megan, who can do it too!" He always tries to be encouraging. Only I'm not sure what he means by "do it," because I never read the dumb thing.

Mom starts to take the book out, but then she puts it back in.

"I'm not going to read on a hike," I say.

"You might want to read it when you're spending the night with Sam's family. Did I tell you that they have their very own cider mill?"

This plan gets worse and worse. And then Mom puts things in my pack: two water bottles, a tube of sunscreen, a bottle of insect repellent, a sketchbook, three charcoal pencils, a pencil sharpener, a rain poncho, and a sweatshirt. Finally she puts this totally stupid baseball cap on my head. It says "I ♥ Vermont" (translation: I Am a Dork!).

Of course I take it right off. "What's all that junk for?"

"These things will come in handy on your hike."

"Two water bottles?"

"There won't be drinking fountains along the trail. And you should never drink water from a stream. You'll get sick."

If I have to carry all that junk, I definitely don't want to go. "Maybe hiking is too dangerous for a girl like me."

Then Dad comes into the kitchen. "What do you mean? Hiking is just what you need. You'll come back with a whole new sense of accomplishment. You'll have a wonderful time. Just think what you'll discover."

I know all I'm going to discover are new ways of being miserable.

"So why don't you take a hike?" I mumble. But like I said, as soon as ART time is over, they'll drive off in the car and they won't be back until tomorrow.

Since I can't drag them along, I decide to bring our dog, Arp. He's sleeping peacefully in his usual spot under the woodstove. I yank him out by the collar and put on his leash. "C'mon. You're going too."

He looks at me like he's saying, "Why are you taking me outside? It's not time to pee."

Arp is a city dog. He's white and fluffy and about the

24

size of a bag of tortilla chips. We've had him since I was in first grade. I wanted to call him Poppleton. But, as usual, nobody listened to me. Instead Dad named Arp after a dumb painter who invented Dada. Dada isn't baby talk. Dada is a bunch of guys who sat around talking about how beautiful painting was a bunch of baloney. I don't get why teachers like Dad think those guys are such geniuses. If I say how dumb everything is, they drag me to museums and make me stare at paintings until I learn to APPRECIATE.

Arp should be on my side, since he hates Vermont as much as I do. But Arp is Mom's baby. He always whines until she picks him up and carries him around. He won't even eat unless she feeds him from her hand. It's disgusting how much nicer she is to him than to me.

Mom puts a bag of dog food in my backpack and hands Ginia a paper bag.

"What am I supposed to eat?" I say.

"Your food is in there too." Mom points to the bag.

"Can't Megan carry her own lunch?" Ginia says.

"It was easier to put everything in the same bag," Mom says.

"But Ginia is such a pig, she'll eat it all," I say.

"I am not!" Ginia says.

"Are too!" I make pig noises.

"Then you carry the lunch," Ginia says.

She shoves the bag at me. It feels so heavy, I'm sorry I said anything. Especially since it won't even be worth carrying. Whatever is in there is sure to be way too healthy and self-improving. But I put it in my backpack.

Sam drives up in his dad's old pickup truck. Ginia runs outside to meet him. They kiss like they haven't seen each other in a zillion years.

It's worse than I thought. The hike is going to be a big, fat slobberfest.

"Mom, please don't make me go with them," I beg her. "You see how they are."

"That's why you have to stay with them. To keep your sister out of trouble," Mom says.

"That is so totally unfair!" I say.

"Sometimes life isn't fair," Mom says.

Like that's going to make me feel better?

She holds up the hat and my backpack. I put on the backpack. I ignore the hat. She sticks it in the backpack as I drag Arp outside.

Ginia leans real close to Sam to whisper. She deliberately does it loud enough so I can hear. "I can't believe she has to come with us. Why should we suffer just because Megan is a lazy slug?"

"Mom!" I wail. "Did you hear what she called me?"

Mom is standing right there, choosing her brushes from the tin can on the back porch. She turns to Ginia like she's going to scold her, but all she says is, "Ginia, don't ignore your sister. Include her."

"I don't want to be included in what they're going to be doing," I say.

"Megan, remember that Ginia is in charge."

The last thing I want is Ginia bossing me. I jerk Arp's leash and stomp down the driveway. I kick a few stones out of my way. I'd rather be kicking Ginia. And then she says in her fake-sweet voice, "Oh, Meggie, you're going the wrong way."

I stop.

"Did you think we were going to hike on the road?" Sam says.

"Actually yes. Because walking on a smooth, flat surface would be the SENSIBLE thing to do!"

Then they all laugh at me. Well, ha, ha, ha.

Sam and Ginia join hands and walk in the other direction. As they stroll past the garden, Sam picks a flower and gives it to Ginia. She acts like it's the most wonderful thing that anyone has ever done. They pass the Hundred-Year-Old Maple and go into the big field that surrounds the farmhouse and the barn. They're about halfway to the Woods, but I'm still standing in the driveway. I'm so angry my feet are burning holes through my shoes.

Mom sighs. "Sweetheart, you're not getting off to a very good start. Can't you try to be more . . ."

The last thing I need is another lecture. "Just leave me alone!"

I drag Arp across the field after Sam and Ginia. As horrible as they are, at least I can count on them to ignore me.

3

Into the Woods

Let me explain something because you might not know
this. If you're a city kid or even a suburb kid, you probably think the Woods are just, like, six trees sticking up
out of the ground the way you drew them in preschool.
Tall, straight trunks topped by a fluffy circle of leaves. A
few friends to make some cool shade or be a backrest for
you if you're sitting down to have a snack.

But that isn't the real Woods. First of all, there are
way more than six trees. There are so many that you
don't even think of them as separate trees that can be
counted. They spread on and on, up over the mountains
and down the other side, on and on until forever. Still, it
wouldn't matter how many there were if they stood in
line like the trees in Central Park. But they don't. They
all crowd together. Their branches are twisted and tangled up. The ground below them is crammed with
smaller trees trying to fight their way up to the sun, and

under those trees are bushes and brambles and weird plants. The trees that have died lie around rotting and hiding under piles of brown leaves, just waiting to trip you. There aren't any paths or spaces to walk. The Woods don't want you to walk in them. And don't forget the swarms of biting insects that hang out there, waiting to suck your blood and give you nasty diseases.

Nothing is worth all that torture. So why would anyone want to go in there? It's not like there's anything fun to do in the Woods. How come Arp and I are the only ones who know that?

Ginia and Sam are almost to Dad's beloved stone wall. But Arp and I have only just started walking in the field. I'm dragging my feet. Actually we can't walk very fast because the grass is taller than Arp. Walking through it is like wading through water. The sun feels warm on my head. The meadow smells nice—not like Ginia's perfume, but clean and good. A yellow butterfly floats above the little blue flowers.

"How about stopping here? This is a good place for lunch."

They ignore me—of course. Ginia is babbling, What's that flower, what's that bird, what's that rock, what's that buzzing, biting insect, like she's going to write a report about this hike. I slow down even more so I won't have to hear her icky little voice say, "Oh, Samster, you know so much about the world." Besides, Arp is pulling me in the other direction. He already took his dump by Mom's precious raspberry bush. He doesn't understand why he can't go back to the farmhouse and have a nap.

Up ahead, the trees look so dark that I start thinking about all the stories I ever read where something goes terribly wrong in the Woods. Kids get lost; witches eat them; trees attack them. You know, people didn't just make that stuff up. They had their reasons. You probably think I'm being ridiculous. Those were old-fashioned times and we live in the twenty-first century. Maybe we do, but the Woods are back in the Dark Ages.

"Oh, Samster, what kind of rocks are those?" Ginia says.

"Heavy ones," Sam says.

What a funny guy.

They're at the stone wall. Dad is sitting beside it on his little camp stool, sketching the rocks so he can paint a different part of the wall. The wall is the boundary between the field and the Woods. But I don't get the point of it. I mean, the wall is only about three feet tall—not nearly high enough to keep any wild animals in the Woods from coming out.

"Bye, Dad," Ginia says.

"Bye, Ginia. Bye, Sam. Be sure to thank your mom for letting my girls spend the night and see your cider mill," Dad says.

"No problem. She loves showing people what real cider's like," Sam says.

"The girls are in for a treat," Dad says.

I can hardly wait. I think the last time I had apple juice was from my sippy cup.

Sam scrambles over the wall and holds out his hand to help Ginia, like it was some huge obstacle or something. Give me a break. If he tries to help me over, I'll slap his hand away. But he doesn't wait. He and Ginia just continue on into the shadowy forest. Her white shorts turn gray. Then Sam and Ginia disappear completely.

I start to yell, "Wait up!" Then I think, What am I doing? Ginia and Sam can rush into the Woods if they want. But if I walk slowly enough, I might never make it to the wall. So I balance on one leg for as long as I can before putting my other foot down. Almost five minutes go by and I've only taken three steps. This is a great plan—until Dad looks up from his sketch.

"Megan, what are you doing?" Dad says.

"Ginia didn't wait and I'm not going in there by myself."

"Ginia, wait for Megan!" Dad yells.

Ginia shouts back, "We'll never get to the beaver dam if we wait for that lazybones!"

"I don't have lazy bones!" I shout.

"That's right. You're nothing but flab!" Ginia yells.

Sam laughs.

"Dad!" I say.

"Your sister's teasing you. Where's your sense of humor?" Dad says.

"Back in New York."

Dad strokes his beard for a moment. "Megan, one of life's many lessons . . ."

At first I think, Oh great. Like I need a lecture right now? Then I think, Oh great! All the time Dad's talking, I'm staying OUT of the Woods.

"Yes, Dad?"

"We don't always have control over our situations. But there is one thing we can control—our minds. Even if you can't change your circumstances, you can always change your attitude."

He's WRONG! I can easily change my circumstances. All I have to do is go back to the house and flop down on the sofa in front of the TV. But it's totally impossible for me to even PRETEND to like hiking in the creepy Woods. And I can never in a million years be nice to Ginia and Sam.

"Why can't I change my attitude driving with you and Mom to Rutland?" I say.

Dad sighs. "Remember the boy in *My Side of the Mountain*? He couldn't wait to run away to the Woods. He had a wonderful time there, living in his tree and eating acorn pancakes."

I'm so sick of that know-it-all book; I want to take it out of my backpack and hit him with it.

"You better hurry. You don't want Ginia to get too far ahead of you." Dad pats me on the back. Then the pat turns into a shove, so I go.

I have to carry Arp over the stone wall. The bright warm sunshine instantly vanishes, like someone flicked a switch. Trees close over my head. It's so much colder out of the sun; I shiver a little. I'm standing on this narrow little gap in the trees that must have been a path for mice or something. This is the hiking trail? This is what Mom has been nagging me to go explore for the past three weeks? This is her idea of fun? But I start walking along it. What else can I do?

"Here we go."

I put Arp down on the path for mice but he jumps against my legs and whines. So I pick him up again. He's warm and soft. It tickles in a nice way as he snuffles at the backpack.

"No, Arp. We aren't having lunch yet."

Actually I'm kind of glad to carry him. I mean, I know I haven't gone very far. Dad's probably still standing there, watching me. There's nothing to be scared of. But the Woods are so, I don't know, dark and solemn, I feel like I don't belong here. It's much worse than the first day of middle school, when I had to walk into a new class all by myself without Lucy.

I go a little faster so I won't think about how weird it is to feel weird. I mean, all I'm doing is walking between a bunch of trees carrying a dog. Arp's leash keeps tangling around my legs, so I take it off.

"Leashes are for dogs that walk."

Arp doesn't get that he should be ashamed of himself.

33

I climb up a little hill. When I look back, I can't see the stone wall anymore. I still can't see Ginia or Sam either. But the mouse path isn't very straight, so it's hard to see too far ahead.

At the bottom of the little hill, Arp starts growling. The hairs stand up all along his back. Oh great, I think. Arp has a bad habit in New York of picking fights. But whatever animal we meet here won't be attached to its owner by a leash. Whatever animal we meet will be wild. And Arp's little growling won't scare anything. It'll just make that animal really annoyed.

"Shut up," I hiss at Arp.

The bushes rustle off to my left.

I hold Arp really tight. I can feel his heart thumping. Mine is pounding too. In fact, they're practically banging into each other.

Then the rustling stops.

"It was probably the wind."

Of course, Arp doesn't say what he thinks. But I decide we better hurry up and find Ginia. So I walk faster up another hill and around a big rock.

"Ginia?" I say softly. I don't want to yell. I don't want her to know I'm starting to panic. She already has enough reasons to humiliate me.

I should have caught up to them by now. Even if I can't see them, I should be hearing her say, "Oh, Samster, what kind of dirt is that?"

Old dead leaves crunch under my feet. I stop walking to listen for Ginia. It's way too unquiet.

This is something else you probably don't know. Everybody is always saying how the city is so noisy. Well, let me tell you, it's the country that is noisy. Maybe it isn't as loud as the city, but it's full of noises. And I don't know for certain what any of them are.

There's a rustle that could be the wind blowing the leaves in the trees. Or it could be an animal creeping through the brush. Or it could be the wings of a huge vulture. There's creaking that could be the branch of a tree about to fall on my head. Or it could be the joints of a huge Bigfoot kind of creature circling me. Normally I don't believe in Bigfoot. It's easy to laugh at him when you're sitting on the sofa, watching a bad home movie of him on TV. But everything is different in the Woods. Even my feelings about wanting to see my sister.

"Ginia?" I call a little louder.

Then I get a news flash. Of course, it's SO obvious. The reason I haven't heard Ginia and Sam is that they're hiding from me. Any moment now, they'll jump out at me. I mean, if they laughed when I got thrown in a pond, then they probably think scaring me would be really hysterical.

"I see you," I say.

Even though I don't.

"Come on, Ginia. This isn't funny."

I hear tittering. I quickly turn toward the sound. Only it isn't Ginia. It's a chipmunk.

Arp barks at it. He tries to get down and chase it. But I hang on tight. Now I'm really getting worried—not about the chipmunk, although even small creatures have teeth that can bite and inject you with disgusting diseases. Something isn't right. Ginia and Sam couldn't have gotten that far ahead. What if something happened to them?

I climb up a bigger hill. But I still can't see Ginia. A pine tree is lying down right along the left side of the path. It's as big as the Christmas tree they put up each year in Rockefeller Center. Its huge mess of roots is taller than I am. And I'm very tall for my age. The tree still has all its green needles, so it makes this long green wall.

I think I should go back and get Dad. *ART* time isn't over yet, so he'll still be at his wall. I think I should tell him that Ginia is lost. Even though Dad's always talking about how great it is to run away to the Woods like that boy did in the book, I know Dad wouldn't think it's great to be LOST.

Then I hear a strange noise coming from beyond the tree. I hold my breath to listen better.

Someone is moaning.

Now I get really worried about Ginia. Anything could have happened to her in the Woods. Maybe the tree fell on her. And then a wild animal attacked her. Or maybe it was a maniac Vermont Fur-Face guy. And Sam didn't save her because HE is the maniac Vermont Fur-Face guy! I tell you, I am so creeped out. I don't want to take another step. But I have to. After all, Ginia is my sister, and she might be good for something when we're older.

I hold Arp even tighter and walk as quietly as I can along the tree. I'm worried that the maniac is still there. The moaning gets louder and louder. Arp shivers a little. I think I'm being extremely brave—as long as I'm hidden by the tree. But then the path curves under the fallen tree, so I have to climb over it. When I get up on top, I see Ginia's legs sticking out from underneath a bush.

I jump down off the tree and hurry toward her. But as I get closer, I hear slurping and smacking of lips. Ginia isn't dying. She's making out with Sam!

I feel like such an idiot. Why did I waste one drop of worry on her? I turn right around and run back toward the path. I'm going straight home to tell Mom and Dad what Ginia is doing. Then she'll be in so much trouble that Mom and Dad will forget all about the Hundred-Year-Old Maple. As I'm sure you know, there's only room for one in the family doghouse.

I'm hurrying as fast as I can, considering that I'm holding a wriggly dog. I want to be sure to make it back to the farmhouse before *ART* time is over and Mom and Dad leave. I'm thinking that as my reward for being the good daughter, they'll definitely take me with them to Rutland. Then *bam*.

I fall flat on my face. Dirt is in my mouth. My hands hurt. My knee is scraped up. I'm in such pain that all I can do is lie there.

"Megan?" Ginia comes out of the bushes and looks over at me.

"What happened?" Sam says.

"Nothing. Megan just tripped. She is such a klutz," Ginia says.

"I wouldn't have tripped if you hadn't been doing disgusting things in the bushes," I say.

"Stop blaming everybody else for your problems," Ginia says.

"I'm not," I say.

"You always do," Ginia says.

"No I don't," I say.

"You're always whining about everything. No wonder Lucy didn't want to spend the summer with you," Ginia says.

I can't believe she said that. My face gets red. And then Sam laughs.

"She did want to," I say.

"That's not what she said," Ginia says.

"She never told you anything," I say.

"I heard her talking on the street to one of her other friends. She said she didn't want to spend the summer watching you lie around and mope," Ginia says.

"I don't lie around and mope," I say.

"That's all I've ever seen you do," Sam says.

"I do plenty of stuff," I say.

"Like whine and complain?" Sam says.

"At least I don't make out in the bushes," I say.

"Nobody would ever make out with you. Nobody wants to be around you. Not even Lucy," Ginia says.

"Shut up shut up shut up!"

But she won't shut up. So I run. Arp's barking. I'm crying. Ginia is shouting. "Megan! Where are you going?"

"I'm going to tell Mom and Dad!"

"Don't you dare!"

"Let her go. At least we're rid of her," Sam says.

I don't hear what Ginia says. I don't care. I hate her. I hate everybody. I hate everybody so much, I hardly notice when I run off the path. Bushes scratch me. Branches whack me. But I keep running as fast as I can. I have to get away from everything, even my own body. I barely feel the bushes or the branches. I can't feel anything except a burning RED RAGE. I run from that too, until I trip and fall again.

Bam! I'm on my face in the dirt. AGAIN. My knees and arms and even the scrapes I got from the Hundred-Year-Old Maple all hurt so much I start to cry.

It isn't fair that I'm always suffering and Ginia gets away with everything. I stagger to my feet. I have to show them. I have to calm down and go back to the farmhouse to tell Mom and Dad how awful Ginia was so she can be grounded forever. But I better hurry, because *ART* time will be over in an hour and Mom and Dad will leave!

I circle back to the path. These trees and bushes keep getting in the way, so I have to go around them. I run a long time. It seems much further than I walked. Only I can't remember how far I walked. I can't remember anything except what Ginia said Lucy said about me.

Finally in the distance I see flickers of light between the trees. The light is off to my left, and not to my right like I think it should be. But I don't care. I know I must be getting near the edge of the Woods. The golden light has to be the sun shining on our field. I'm so tired, but I start running again. Now my heart is pounding in triumph. I made it back. I didn't get lost in the Woods.

I check my watch. It's only eleven-thirty. It's still *ART* time. Mom and Dad haven't left yet. They can still take me with them to Rutland.

"Mom! Dad! I have to go with you. I'm not staying with Ginia. She's so disgusting and mean. You won't believe what she did!"

I burst from the gloom and into sunlight so bright that it blinds me for a moment. I run through a field of daisies and those orange flowers that Ginia always picks for Mom because Sam told her they're called Indian paintbrushes.

Then I stop.

What happened to the barn and the farmhouse? Where's the stone wall? Where's the Hundred-Year-Old Maple? I turn around and around again, thinking somehow I'm just not seeing them. They have to be here, right? Who could have taken them?

A buzz of insects swells until the roar fills my head. I sink onto the ground. But I can't catch my breath. My heart won't stop racing.

This isn't the field by the farmhouse. This is a field I've never been to in my whole life.

4
The Appalachian Trail

I stay there like that for I don't know how long. Forever, I think. Much longer than I ever sat staring at the blank TV screen. But no one gets mad at me for doing nothing. No one tells me to get some exercise. No one calls me lazybones. No one is there.

And I mean no one.

I've been on my own plenty of times before, waiting for my parents to get home from teaching. But when I'm by myself in our apartment, I can hear the upstairs neighbors moving around above my head. I can look out the window and see people walking by on the street. I can turn on the TV and find people there.

But now I'm the only human anywhere. It's like everybody in the whole world abandoned me because they really don't want to see me lie around and mope. I hate thinking that. I shut my eyes so I won't have to see how all alone I am.

I keep lying there, even though dry weeds poke my back and creepy bugs crawl across my legs. I'm too exhausted to even lift my hand to brush them away. Besides, what's the point of getting up? Even if I somehow stagger to my feet, I'll still be in a field in Vermont with absolutely ZERO idea of how to get back to the farmhouse. And even if I figure out how to get back, why on Earth should I go where everybody hates me?

This is it. The end.

I lie there, sinking deeper into darkness. But no one cares.

Then I hear the sound of jingling dog tags coming toward me. So I open my eyes. There's Arp, running across the field as fast as his little legs can go.

When he jumps on me and licks my face, I start sobbing. Now you know how bad off I am if dog slobber seems like a good thing.

I hug him so tight I'm practically strangling him. He wriggles out of my arms and jumps around. He wags his stubby tail so hard he almost falls over.

"Were you lost and worried too?"

He barks like he's trying to tell me all about it. I pat him. His white fur is all dirty and full of burrs.

"Look at you. You're such a mess! But you found me, didn't you? Yes you did, you good dog."

He looks so pleased with himself. I don't have the heart to tell him that even though we've found each other, we're still lost.

"Hey, Arp. You think you can sniff your way back to the farmhouse?"

Arp sits down, like he's saying, "Hey! I just got here."

"It can't be very far. We didn't walk that long. Did we?"

He pants so much his pink tongue dangles way out of his mouth.

"We just have to go back the way we came."

But which way did we come from? I look around, trying to remember where I first ran into the field. But I can't see a sign or even that path for mice. The field is totally surrounded by the Woods. Yes, the same old Woods. I told you they go on forever.

Arp gazes up at me, like I'm supposed to know what to do.

"What are you looking at me for? You're the dog. You're the one with the good sense of smell. How am I supposed to know which direction to go in?"

Of course, Samster would know, just by the color of the moss on the tree bark. Or where the sun is in the sky. I check my watch to see what time it is. It seems like a whole lifetime went by since Ginia said what she said about Lucy.

It's one o'clock. *ART* time is over. My parents are on their way to Rutland. They don't even know I'm lost.

This is so depressing that I fall back onto the ground. But then I realize something. Nobody is at the farmhouse. When I get back there, I can finish off the Ben & Jerry's Chunky Monkey ice cream and watch TV. Maybe the sound still works even without the rabbit-ear antenna.

The sun is sort of straight overhead. I squint at it through my fingers; I have enough problems without getting blind from looking directly at the sun. Finally it moves.

I jump up and shout, "Okay, Arp! That's west!"

Arp looks at me like he's saying, "What's all the fuss?" So I explain it to him, since he never had science class. "The sun sets in the west. So the sun has to move that way."

I don't tell him that the sun isn't really moving; the Earth is. (That's hard enough for people to understand.) I just point toward the right side of the field and say, "That's west."

Unfortunately I still have no idea where the farm-house is.

We spent all that time studying maps in school. We learned how to mark off five blocks east, two blocks south, three more blocks east to get from the pretend playground to the pretend library. That method works really well in New York City because it's a sensible, organized place with numbered streets in the right order. But the Woods aren't measured out in little boxes. The Woods are even more out of control than Ginia.

I start getting upset again.

45

Arp barks.

"Don't blame me," I tell him. "I KNEW that hiking in the Woods was a terrible idea. I KNEW that a bad thing was going to happen. But did anybody listen to me? No. And now I'm dying out here because my family didn't care about me—they cared about a TREE. My very own family! You know, the ones that have the same blood as I do? Like, hello, people? In case you didn't notice, I am a people too. And that means I have a brain and feelings, but plants don't."

Just to prove that, I drop to my knees and pull up huge clumps of grass.

"You see? Did they get mad or say ouch? No. You see? No feelings!"

I throw the grass. Only it doesn't go far away like I want it to. The grass just floats around and lands on my legs. That makes me mad. Like the plants are doing that on purpose to bug me. And if they are, that means they do have little minds. So I quickly brush off the grass.

"Leave me alone!" I tell it.

"Leave" reminds me of leaves. Like I made a pun. Now I feel even worse. You see, Lucy and I love puns. We spend hours making them. If Lucy were there, she would say, "Leaf you alone?"

Then I would say, "Stop being corny."

And she would say, "Seed ya later."

On and on forever, laughing because it's fun to be laughing. Who cares if the jokes are lame?

46

But I haven't laughed at all since I came to Vermont. Okay, maybe I laughed on the inside when I was torturing my family. But that doesn't count. When you laugh by yourself, the laughter just ends. You need two people for an extravaganza of laughing. And not just any old person. Believe me, Ginia is NOT the type to bounce it back. So I haven't had a great laugh since the last time I saw Lucy. Actually not even then, because Lucy didn't laugh much in sixth grade.

Now that I think about it, our last great laugh was way back in September before anybody ever even heard of Hodgkin's lymphoma. Lucy and I were planning our Halloween costumes. We always planned months ahead, because you have to if you want a truly phenomenal costume. Lucy wanted us to be Inside-out People and wear our clothes inside out. But that seemed a little boring. So I said we should have our hearts and lungs and stomachs all outside our skin. Then Lucy said to be really and truly inside out, we'd have to show what was IN our hearts and lungs and stomachs. "And our colons!" I said. That started one of the biggest laughs of all time.

Those costumes would have been so cool, we probably would have gotten our pictures in the *Daily News*. Only they never happened. Alison wanted to help us, like she has every year since Lucy and I were butterflies in kindergarten. But Alison was so tired all during October. Some days she couldn't even get out of bed. I told Lucy that my mom could do it. Alison should just rest and get better. (That was when we all thought she had the flu.) But my mom—who ought to have been clever with her fingers, since she calls herself an artist—said our idea was too complicated for her to make. By then it was too late to be brilliant. Lucy was a gypsy and I was a clown. Our outfits didn't match at all. So nobody knew we were together. When we were walking to the neighborhood parade, we ran into Patricia Palombo. She was a gypsy too. But she didn't get mad and call Lucy a copycat. She said, "Ooh, Lucy! We can be from the same tribe!" Then she made Lucy walk with her and I had to follow along behind.

Patricia Palombo is such an idiot. Gypsies don't have tribes. Gypsies have, well, I don't know what, only I know they DON'T have tribes.

I lie down in the field again. The sun is burning me. The dried grass is poking me. The bugs are crawling on me. I'm kind of feeling sorry for myself. Kind of? Okay. I'm TOTALLY feeling sorry for myself.

Then I hear a voice. It isn't Arp. It isn't my fairy godmother. It's that good old yucky you-can't-do-it voice.

"You SHOULD feel sorry for yourself. You're the most PATHETIC person ever made. You should have a permanent L on your forehead. You can't do anything except doodle. You're bad at sports. You don't get good grades. Your hair is frizzy. Your clothes are ugly. You look fat in them."

The yucky voice goes on and on. The list of stuff I'm bad at is endless.

I put my hands over my ears. That doesn't help. I'm lost and abandoned. Even after someone finds me, Ginia will never let me forget the day I was too dumb to find my way out of the Woods.

"But that's not fair. It's all Ginia's fault." I jump up and yell, "Come on, Arp! What are you doing lying there feeling sorry for yourself? If we get going, Ginia will never know we were lost."

I put on my backpack and stomp across the field. He runs after me. I kind of think I'm heading back the way I came. But to be honest, I don't really know. All those trees look alike.

This time I'm glad to get out of the sun. At least it's cool in the shade. The crawling bugs and buzzing flies are gone. Even the yucky voice is quiet. Of course, there are other kinds of insects. Mostly whining mosquitoes, but they only bother me when I stop walking.

Pretty soon, I find a path that is like a trail for rabbits instead of mice. We follow it for a while, until it runs into another path that looks like it's really going somewhere, so we walk on it. Unfortunately that path ends, so we have to go back to what I think is the other path, only I'm not exactly sure. Arp sniffs like he recognizes it, but it turns out he's just looking for a place to pee. When I try to look ahead, all I can see are green leaves.

49

"How am I supposed to see where I'm going with all these stupid trees in the way?"

The yucky voice says, *"The trees aren't stupid, you are."* But then I hear some real live humans talking.

"Did you hear that, Arp? It's the rescue party. HELLO!" I shout.

Then I remember that I don't want Ginia to know how lost I was, so I just casually—but quickly—run through the Woods toward the voices.

At the top of a hill, there's a path. It's like a four-lane superhighway compared to that little winding thing I was on. The tree closest to me is marked with a rectangular splotch of blue paint. There's another mark on another tree halfway down the hill. I don't know what the splotches mean; I just know that people made them. And that means civilization.

By the third mark, at the foot of the hill, I see a woman and a man hiking up toward me. They're both wearing backpacks. I used to think my sixth-grade backpack was big and heavy when it was full of homework, but these packs are so huge that junk actually sticks up above these people's heads. The woman is wearing a floppy sun hat and carrying a long walking stick. I can't see the man very well because he's behind her. The path is wide enough to walk side by side. But they don't. They're arguing.

"Stop saying that," the woman says.

"Don't tell me what to do. Besides, it's true," the man says.

They don't sound at all like a rescue party. I pick up Arp and hug him so he won't be too disappointed. Then I think the people might be able to help us anyway, so we wait for them to get closer.

"You don't have to go on and on about it," the woman says.

"I thought you'd be glad to know you've hiked one thousand five hundred eighty-seven miles of the Appalachian Trail," the man says.

"How could I possibly be glad when I still have five hundred ninety-one miles to go?"

You've probably never heard of the Appalachian Trail, unless you have parents like mine. One day, after *ART* time, Mom and Dad were going to take Ginia and me to walk on it a little. "Then you can say you've hiked on the Appalachian Trail," Mom said. I was all confused because I thought the mountains in Vermont were called the Green Mountains. Then Dad explained that the Green Mountains are part of the Appalachian Mountains and the Trail goes through the mountains all the way from Georgia to Maine. I still didn't see why Mom was so excited about walking on it. Anyway, it rained that day, so we went to visit Calvin Coolidge's house instead. You probably never heard of him either, but he was a Vermont guy back in the twentieth century who

51

got to be president when the real president died.

Halfway up the hill, the man sits on a nice big rock and takes off his pack.

The woman stops too, but she doesn't sit or take off her pack. "What are you doing? We had lunch already."

"It's time for a snack."

After the man searches through his pack for a while, the woman says with a little smirk, "I took out your Double Stuf Oreos."

The man gets all red in the face. "What? How could you do that to me?"

"Cookies are empty, useless calories. You didn't even get the peanut butter kind."

"I don't like Nutter Butters. Besides, they were in MY pack!"

"They take up space so we can't divide the rest of the food evenly."

"I don't care; I need them. Where did you put them? You couldn't have thrown them away."

He's right. There aren't any trash cans in the Woods.

"I left them at the shelter where we slept last night," the woman says.

"Then I'm going back to get them," the man says.

"Five miles? We'll lose the entire day."

"I need something sweet to keep me going."

"You can go back if you want to. But I'm not doing

those miles again. We've got six more to do today." The woman continues up the hill.

The man sighs and then grunts as he lifts his pack up onto his shoulders.

"I wish you had joined that other group at Mount Greylock," he says.

Mount Greylock? I can't believe it! Mount Greylock is the mountain you can see from Mrs. T.'s window with the stone tower and the souvenir store on top. That's probably where the man bought the Double Stuf Oreos.

But had these people climbed it? Had they walked here from there?

Now the woman is about ten feet from where I'm standing. So I ask her. "Excuse me. Did you really walk here all the way from Mount Greylock?"

"Of course. It's only thirty miles away," the woman says.

"Thirty-two miles," the man says.

"Mount Greylock, Massachusetts?" I say.

"Is there another one?" the woman says.

"If you had left me there, I'd still have my Double Stuf Oreos," the man says.

"I hope I don't have to hear about those Double Stuf Oreos for the next five hundred ninety miles!" the woman says.

"Five hundred ninety-one miles," the man says.

"Will you shut up?" the woman says.

"Why did you want to hike the Appalachian Trail in the first place?"

"It's a test. If I can hike the Appalachian Trail with you, I can do anything."

"What's that supposed to mean?"

"What do you think?"

They're still arguing as they disappear around a bend. The trees make a tunnel of green that goes all the way to Maine. But I look in the other direction, through the tunnel of green that leads to Mount Greylock and Lucy.

"Can you believe those people really walked all the way from Georgia? Georgia is practically at the other end of the United States. Compared to Georgia, Massachusetts is right next door."

I put Arp down and pat his head.

"If those old people could walk all the way from Georgia, we can certainly walk thirty miles to Mount Greylock. Then we could see Lucy!"

Arp whaps my leg with his tail. He doesn't really care. He's only happy because I sound happy. And I am. Thinking about Lucy makes me feel a whole lot better. It's going to be so great to see her—whenever that is. She'll laugh when I tell her how Ginia almost made me believe that Lucy didn't want to visit me. She'll call Ginia a big liar. Then Lucy will swear she never told anyone that she didn't want to watch me lie around and mope.

"But we aren't lying around moping right now, are we? We're on the Appalachian Trail."

I stomp my foot down on the dirt for emphasis. Then I walk a few steps in a really goofy way. "See? I'm hiking it."

It's too bad Lucy isn't here to laugh. Arp barks, but he doesn't really get the joke.

"Maybe we should hike to Mount Greylock. That would show them."

Just so you know, I'm only kidding around. Here's a good clue for you: I AM TALKING TO A DOG.

This dog isn't a Loyal Dog that you can have a real discussion with. Loyal Dogs are big and brown. Their wise eyes look at you like you're the most wonderful person in the world and whatever you say is pure genius. If you have a Loyal Dog, then you can walk thirty miles to Mount Greylock. But Arp is no Loyal Dog. He's little and fluffy and dirty white. And (I'm kind of embarrassed to mention this) he has a ponytail sticking up on the top of his head. That's because his fur flops in his eyes. Mom wanted to cut it but Dad was afraid Arp would look like a sissy dog. (Hello, Dad? Arp IS a sissy dog.) So no haircuts. But Mom felt sorry for Arp in the hot summer. So she took one of Ginia's scrunchies and made a little ponytail on his forehead.

"Come here, Arp." I pull off the scrunchie. I'm going to use my finger like a gun to shoot it off into the Woods. But instead I use it to pull my hair back. Usually I don't wear ponytails because they make my hair stick out in a funny way, but it feels much cooler to have the hair off the back of my neck.

"There." After I muss up the fur on his forehead, he looks a whole lot more like a dog you can trust.

"I'm sure we can easily hike to Mount Greylock or maybe even Georgia because you and I are such terrific hikers."

Arp is supposed to say something like "Yeah right." Only he doesn't seem to know I'm kidding. He wags his tail and barks at me. Then he starts down the hill.

"Hey! Where do you think you're going?"

I stand there with my mouth hanging open until he turns to look back at me. He cocks his head to one side like he's saying, "Are you coming or not?" Then he trots along the Appalachian Trail toward Mount Greylock.

What can I do? I run after him. It's bad enough being the second girl in the family and always following behind Ginia and even Lucy sometimes. But I absolutely refuse to walk behind a little dog whose tail sticks up so you can see his butthole.

When I catch up to him, I say, "Okay. We'll hike to Mount Greylock. But remember, I'm the leader."

5
The Shelter

That's how Arp and I start hiking the Appalachian Trail.

Since the Trail is much wider than the paths we were on, no bushes scratch me. No branches poke me. The trees make a roof above my head that feels kind of protective, if you know what I mean. Like they aren't going to let anything bad happen to Arp or me. So we just walk along. When I see a nice straight branch about four feet long on the ground next to the Trail, I pick it up. I don't really need a walking stick, but carrying it makes me feel like a professional.

This hiking is so easy; I can't understand why people make such a fuss about it. Walking in New York City is much harder. If you want a real challenge, you should try Times Square—especially on matinee day. Whenever Mrs. T. takes Lucy and me to see a Broadway show, we have to fight our way through the mobs and dodge around the people selling hot dogs and drawings of your name in flowered letters. Big crowds always gather around street performers. I can see why you might be interested in the Naked Cowboy. But why do tourists stand around and stare at the people who aren't doing anything except pretending to be statues? When the crowds get too big, we have to leave the sidewalk and walk right on Forty-second Street. The streets are crazy with cabs honking horns and bicycle messengers riding in the wrong direction and long white limos that never have a famous person in them, just someone from New Jersey. If you stop for one second to look in the window of the Hello Kitty store, a wave of people carries away your friends. Then you have to run to catch up, and hope you don't get whacked by briefcases or burnt by the cigarettes people hold since they can't smoke inside any buildings.

But there's nothing here except different kinds of green for miles and miles. The only people I meet are walking their golden retriever. They say hello. The dogs sniff each other's butts. Then Arp and I keep going. We're traveling pretty fast, since it's mainly downhill.

"We're in luck. Our trip will probably be downhill all the way, since Mount Greylock, Massachusetts, is south of Vermont and south is below us on the map."

Of course, Arp doesn't get my joke. I don't care. I'm feeling so much better about everything now. Don't tell my mom, but after a whole summer of doing nothing, it actually feels good to hike along the Trail. Finally I'm getting somewhere. Each time my foot hits the dirt, I'm one step further away from Ginia and one step closer to Lucy.

This is my plan: Arp and I will hike five miles to that shelter. We'll spend the night there, feasting on the Double Stuf Oreos that woman left behind. Tomorrow we'll hike the rest of the way to Mount Greylock. I'll buy ice cream and other delicious things at the souvenir store with the ten dollars in my backpack and eat them for lunch. Then I'll call Lucy. She'll be so glad to see me that she won't be mad at me for complaining about having slime in my hair. I won't even have to ask her if she really said that all I do is lie around and mope, since I'll have proved that's not true. Then I'll call my parents, who will be back from Rutland by then. They'll make Ginia apologize. And everybody will be very impressed that I hiked the whole way and even climbed Mount Greylock.

"How did you do it?" Lucy will say.

And I'll say, "Oh it was easy."

The only problem is, it isn't easy anymore.

Now Arp and I are mostly going uphill. That isn't good because of this thing called gravity that always wants to drag you down. I consider following a littler trail that's NOT going up against gravity. But I'm afraid to leave the blue splotches. I don't want to be lost again.

Pretty soon I'm panting as much as Arp. My backpack is so heavy that while I climb, it tries to tip me over backward and make me roll all the way down the hill.

"What did Mom put in here?" Then I remember. I was so excited about not being lost and hiking to Lucy that I forgot to eat lunch. "That's our problem, Arp. We're hungry!"

I sit right down on a big gray rock and open up my pack. There's a bag of kibble and a few dog treats. At first Arp looks at me like I should hold it for him in my hand the way Mom does. But I don't have time for that. "I'm hungry too," I say.

I put his food on the rock, and guess what? He gobbles it up.

I open the paper bag with my lunch. As I suspected, it's terrible. There's a bag of purple grapes that's been in the refrigerator for weeks. There are four long unpeeled carrots. There are four peanut butter sandwiches on awful whole wheat bread with that seedy raspberry jam that only Ginia likes. There are two oatmeal-raisin granola bars. There's a package of trail mix. I immediately pick out all six M&M'S and eat them. But most of it is nuts and weird dried brown things that might be fruit. It's a total waste of money, since the ratio of good stuff to bad is about 1 to 100. Wouldn't it be more economical to buy a whole big bag of M&M'S? And if Mom really thinks creativity is so important, then why did she give me plain old ordinary boring water? I'm so thirsty I drink some. But even Arp prefers to lap up the water from a little puddle, because at least the dirt gives it a flavor. As bad as all that is, you won't believe what's at the bottom of the lunch bag. A plastic package of something so brown and slimy, I have to read the label to find out what it is. Barbecued tofu strips! Is Mom trying to kill me or what?

The only thing that saves me is the thought of those Double Stuf Oreos waiting for me in that shelter. I eat half a sandwich and take another sip of water. Then I jump up and put on my pack. "Come on, Arp."

He's having a nap. His belly is full of delicious dog food. But I'm still starving to death because Mom doesn't care enough about me to give me something besides disgusting health food. And Dad doesn't care enough to keep her from starving me. And Ginia, well, you know how much Ginia cares about me.

If they don't care about me, I sure won't care about them. I won't worry that they might bo worried. They won't be. Not one bit. By now Mom and Dad are probably eating popcorn in a movie theater in Rutland. And Ginia and Sam are enjoying their uninterrupted slobberfest. Who needs them anyway? Not me. I'm hiking to Mount Greylock to see my best friend, Lucy.

"Come on, Arp."

I tap him with my stick when he won't wake up.

He growls at me. But I don't care. I nudge him a little harder.

"We have to get to that shelter, so come on!"

He gets up, turns in a circle, and lies back down again.

"Okay, fine! I'll go without you!"

I start hiking. I hope I'll get back that feeling I had when I first started going to Mount Greylock. But I don't. I'm so mad at everyone, I don't even speak to Arp when he catches up to me. I rub my eyes to wipe away some liquid that is leaking from under my eyelids. So I guess I'm not exactly watching where I'm going. But still, that branch shouldn't be leaning over the Trail. It almost pokes my eye out. I whack the branch with my stick to move it out of the way. Whacking feels so good, I keep on whacking, even though swinging my arms gets me out of breath. I name the trees I whack. If it has oozing sap like fake tears, it's Mom. Dad has peeling bark like how he's losing his hair. But the ones with gnarly parts are Ginia. I give them double whacks.

After a million whacks, I check my watch. It's five o'clock. Any minute now, I'm sure I'll see that shelter. The woman said it was only five miles back. I know I hiked way more than five. My legs are so wobbly, I feel like I've hiked all the way to Georgia. I can't go another step. I don't even walk to a nice rock. I plop down on the dirt. Arp lies down next to me.

"Are you sure you can hike all that way?" It's the yucky you-can't-do-it voice.

"What if you don't find that shelter? How do you even know there is a shelter? Are you sure the Double Stuf Oreos are still there? What if somebody else ate them?"

I cover my ears.

62

"What are you going to do when it gets DARK?"

"SHUT UP!" I shout.

But the voice won't shut up, so I pick up my pack and keep going.

Trees, trees, trees, dead tree, trees, trees, trees, bush, trees, trees, trees, rock.

"Arp? Where is that shelter?"

Now it's almost seven o'clock.

Dinner would be over. Of course, even if I were at the farmhouse, I'd still be starving. Now that we're in Vermont, dinner is usually something like a plate of heirloom tomatoes and goat cheese salad. Only tonight, Mom and Dad are eating with their friends, who probably cook normal food like hamburgers because they aren't trying to "embrace nature and live where they are."

Arp sits down again.

"I'm tired and hungry too, but we aren't having dinner or resting or anything until we get to that shelter."

I have another reason for wanting to get there in a hurry. It's too embarrassing to say. Just remember I'm not a dog who doesn't care where he lifts his leg to go.

Then I hear this heavy breathing coming up behind us on the Trail.

I freeze. I know I should hide in the bushes because you can't be too careful when you're a girl alone in the Woods and your Loyal Dog is only about one foot tall. But I don't have time for that. I look over my shoulder and see a man with a glistening red face and bulging eyes running toward me. At first, I think, Oh no! But then I notice he's wearing running shorts and a T-shirt that says TAKE A HIKE—Up a Mountain. He's not a maniac; he's a fitness nut. And I do mean NUT, because he runs UP the hill!

"Hey, Mister, have you seen a shelter?"

"No," he says as he passes me.

"Are you sure?"

"Can't stop. Training to climb peaks."

He disappears over the top of the hill.

Arp and I just stand there with our tongues hanging out. (To be honest, Arp's tongue is always hanging out.) But neither of us can believe he RAN up the hill when we can barely lift our feet to take one more step.

"Come on," I say. I have to go really badly now.

But Arp won't come on. So I pick him up. Somehow I stagger to the top. I put Arp down. And guess what? He immediately goes chasing off after a chipmunk. I'm so mad at him, especially after I carried him all that way. But I'm worried he'll get lost, so I yell at him. "Get back here!"

The strangest thing happens as I watch him run along the top of the ridge. This blaze of light makes him glow.

"Look what the sun's doing." It seems kind of cool—until I realize—"Oh no. Look what the sun's doing!"

I haven't been keeping careful track of the sun

because I had other stuff to worry about. But now I climb up on a boulder to get a better view. The sun isn't above me anymore. It's way off to my right, sitting on top of the trees. And it isn't yellow either. It's bright orange. That's when I discover the real reason for sunsets. It isn't about how pretty the clouds look. Those colors aren't trying to inspire Dad to broaden his palette. They're warning you that DARK IS COMING! You better find whatever you need because pretty soon you won't be able to see it.

I jump off the boulder. DARK is already spreading out from the trees. As it spreads, it will erase the Woods and the Trail and eventually even me.

"Come on, Arp. We've got to find that shelter."

I'm so panicky I start running along the Trail, just like the fitness nut.

I HATE the DARK! Don't tell anybody, but I didn't sleep at all my first nights in Vermont because of the darkness. The night sky in New York City doesn't get black; it turns kind of purple because of all the street-lights and lights in buildings and lights on buildings. The only DARK you can find in New York City is if you are standing on the subway platform and you look deep into the tunnel. So I didn't even know DARK creeped me out until I got to Vermont. Of course, eleven and three-quarters is way too old to have a problem like that. I even considered putting a night-light in my room, but then Ginia would have added one more thing to her list of stuff to tease me about.

Believe me, I'm not looking forward to spending the night in the dark Woods listening to the yucky voice say, *"I told you it would get DARK and you'd never find the shelter or the Double Stuf Oreos."*

I hurry so much that I run right past the shelter!

I'm all the way down one hill and halfway up the next before it hits me. That pathetic pile of boards back there on the side of the hill—that's the shelter?

I walk back to it. I mean, what else can I do?

The shelter has a wooden floor and a wooden roof. But it doesn't have four walls, which I thought was standard for all buildings. It only has two.

"What's the problem here? Did whoever built it forget to put up the other two walls? Or did he get tired and quit with the job half finished?"

Arp doesn't know. He sits down and scratches his ear.

"This shelter isn't even as good a house as the first little pig made. The wolf wouldn't even have to blow anything down—all he'd have to do is walk right in."

Obviously if you don't have enough walls, then you don't have a door that can be shut and locked to keep out wild animals.

I climb up on the platform. The two walls meet in a corner. In that corner, there are two more wooden platforms for beds. That's it. No soft chairs, no electricity, no running water, no cupboards to store packages of Double Stuf Oreos. And NO BATHROOM!

I don't know what to do, so I sit on a platform. I'm so

tired my head droops down. But looking at the floor is a big mistake. It's filthy. The wooden boards are covered with trash and leaves. And then I notice about a zillion of those little black dots that, after living in Vermont, I've learned are mouse poop.

I get out of there fast and go sit on a nearby rock. I mean, I know the mice are in the Woods. But mice are supposed to be outside because they are ANIMALS. And I'm supposed to be inside lying on a nice soft bed watching TV because I'm a HUMAN!

However, that's not the situation here.

And by the way, where are those Double Stuf Oreos anyway? From where I sit, I can see they aren't under the platforms. And there isn't any other place they could be.

I just sit there, slapping the mosquitoes on my arms and legs, staring at the shelter. Now what? The more I stare at it, the worse I feel. It's such a rip-off. In fact, this whole summer is the biggest rip-off ever. And I WANT MY MONEY BACK!

Only I won't get it. I won't get anything I want. Ever. And there isn't anything I can do about it except—you guessed it—cry.

Arp comes over to see what I'm doing. I try to snuffle up my tears because I'm supposed to be his leader and leaders don't cry. Only he knows. He cocks his head to one side and looks at me really sadly.

"Oh, Arp. How are we ever going to make it to Mount Greylock?"

He puts his paw on my foot.

"How are we going to get through the night with only half a shelter and not one single Double Stuf Oreo?"

Our situation is totally hopeless. But one thing can't wait a single second longer. Even though the shelter doesn't have a bathroom, I have to go.

I look at Arp. He isn't giving any advice on the subject. Besides, he's a boy dog, so that makes everything easier for him.

One thing I know is: don't go too near the shelter. I hurry over to a clump of bushes. I can imagine that the leaves are very realistic wallpaper, but it's a lot harder to imagine the toilet.

"You know, Arp, there was a time when nobody had toilets."

I shouldn't have spoken to him, because he trots over to see what I'm doing.

"Don't look!" I yell at him. I don't want him to see me with my pants down. But I shouldn't have gotten mad at him. He's not going to laugh at my flowered underwear like certain girls do when I change into my uniform for gym class.

It's done. I did it. And let me tell you, I feel so much better. I practically skip back to the shelter.

Then the most amazing thing happens.

I see a monarch butterfly.

Okay, I know you're thinking, So what? Everybody sees butterflies. What's the big deal?

But have you ever really looked at a butterfly? They're the most rinky-dink contraptions. Their wings are just like paper. They don't have any solid bones or anything. They aren't streamlined like birds. They aren't strong. They can't even fly in a straight line. They flutter. They flutter by. But that little thing that seems like it won't make it from a tree to a bush, that little thing flies all the way from Mexico to Vermont. They really do. Dad told me that when I was still paying attention to his lectures. They don't have maps or trails or food or shelters. But they do it. Every single year. Then, like that wasn't hard enough, they fly back again! And they don't have bathrooms either.

So I decide I better get a grip. I mean, do I have to be such an idiot? No, I don't. Sometimes I pretend to be dumb to make Lucy laugh. But I'm really sort of smart. At least that's what Mom and Dad and my teachers always tell me. They say, "Come on, Megan, you're smart enough to know better." Well, guess what? Maybe I really can figure out what I'm doing. I solved the bathroom problem, didn't I? So now all I have to do is clean the shelter.

"Come on, Arp. We've got work to do. I'm not sleeping in mouse poop!"

Kicking those little turds doesn't work very well. But a pine branch makes a pretty good broom. I sweep the platforms and the floor and pick up all the trash. There sure are a lot of beer cans. I practically cry when I see the empty potato chip bags. But I don't find any Double Stuf Oreo wrappers. There isn't a garbage can or anything, so I dump the trash over where other people had built fires. When the shelter is as clean as I can get it, I pile up pine needles on the platform for my bed. They smell just like Christmas. But when I sit on them, they're really scratchy.

"Too bad we don't have something to put over them."

Then I remember the poncho Mom packed in my backpack. It's so dorky that I wouldn't be caught dead in it, no matter how hard it rained. For one thing, it's the color of old-lady underwear. But it can cover the pine needles. I also find a sweatshirt and insect repellent. I put the sweatshirt right on because I'm getting cold. Then I spritz insect repellent everywhere because darkness brings out mosquito vampires who suck your blood.

Of course, when Arp sees me go in the backpack, he runs over with his tail wagging.

"You ate all your dog biscuits." But I give him a carrot. After I eat the rest of the peanut butter sandwich, he's glad to gobble up the crusts. Then I drink the rest of one water bottle. And he finds a nice muddy puddle.

I'm still hungry, but I decide to save the other sandwiches for tomorrow. And no way will I eat anything with nuts in it. I look deeper in the backpack. Maybe there's a candy bar or something. I would have gladly eaten old Halloween candy. But instead I find a folded-up piece of paper.

It's a note from Lucy. It has my name written on the outside in her handwriting. She used her pen with the purple ink that she saves for special occasions.

I just hold it for a long time with both hands. "Arp, this is from Lucy."

He isn't very impressed. He just gives it the smallest sniff when I hold it under his nose.

"Don't you realize how amazing it is? It's like Lucy is here with us right now telling us something very important."

I stop trying to get him interested. After all, she's my best friend, not his. I slowly open up the letter.

This is Lucy's message to me as I continue on my journey:

What should I do about my hair?

Well, okay, really the note is from last November, when Lucy was deciding whether or not to let her hair grow. I wanted her to keep it short because that was how it always was. But Patricia Palombo and some of the other girls thought it would look cuter long. Lucy was torn, even though she shouldn't have listened to them, since they weren't her best friends. So I had drawn a picture of her to show her how fabulous short hair could look.

It was a cartoon, since I can't draw people that look like people. Still, I got her smile the way it is when she's thinking up a fun plan for us. But I messed up her hair.

71

That's why I never gave her the picture. It didn't matter anyway. After Alison got cancer, Lucy cut her hair so short, she looked like a boy.

I wonder how her hair is now. It seems like such a long time since I saw her.

I fold the paper up again. It makes me sad, so I start to put it away. And then I see Lucy has written another message on the back.

you've got a friend
climb every mountain
circle of Love

I'm crying now. Lucy is so smart. She saw into the future and knew what I would need to keep me going. I wipe my eyes and keep reading.

give my regards to broadway
rudolph the red-nosed reindeer

Well, okay, so maybe she just wrote down a list of songs the chorus was going to sing. But maybe she knew. Maybe she knows.

I take out a pencil and fix the drawing. I make her hair a little bit longer. Then I make her smile a little bit bigger. I draw Arp and me right beside her, like we just arrived and she's really glad to see us. I make a cartoon bubble so she can say, "I'M SO GLAD YOU'RE HERE!" I make another bubble so Arp can say, "WOOF!" Then I make one last bubble so I can say, "WE MADE IT!"

I look at the picture for a long time. Even as the darkness settles in around us so that I can hardly see anything except the white piece of paper.

It's time for bed.

I carefully fold up the drawing and put it in my backpack. Then I put my backpack on the platform so it can be a pillow. Arp jumps up to give it one last sniff. Then he sighs and plops down in the middle of my bed.

"Arp! Where am I supposed to sleep?"

He doesn't make any suggestions.

I curl myself around him so he doesn't have to move. I put my head on my backpack. And do you know what I see when I look over at the post that holds up the roof in the opposite corner?

A clear plastic grocery store bag dangles by its handles from a nail just a little below the ceiling. And even though it's seriously getting dark now, through the bag I can just barely make out the letters O R E O S.

Oh, Oreos, dear Double Stuf Oreos. The dark chocolate cookie, the creamy white double fluff. Oh, Oreos, dear Double Stuf Oreos, now I'm truly saved.

I'm so tired, I don't get them right away. I fall asleep with them floating up there above me like a beautiful dream.

6
Thank Goodness for Oreos!

Do you think I sleep peacefully the rest of the night?

Boy, are you wrong.

Lots of things keep waking me up. In the first place, I'm not lying on a thick mattress that's covered with a soft purple flannel sheet. In fact, I'm lying on the COMPLETE OPPOSITE of that. An anti-bed. There's nothing harder than wood and nothing scratchier than pine needles. Even the rain poncho that seemed like such a good idea before is sticky and useless. So you can forget all about being comfortable.

Still, I'm so totally exhausted from all my hiking that I shouldn't care that I'm on an anti-bed. But every time I shut my eyes, I hear a whiny buzzing sound that means a million mosquitoes are coming to attack. I know you think, How can that be? She put on lots of insect repellent. That's right, I did. Only maybe next time I hike the

Appalachian Trail, Mom won't try to be so environmentally correct and will give me some spray that actually kills.

After the mosquitoes move on because there isn't any blood left in me to suck, Arp starts having doggy dreams. The rabbits are just in his head, but his little legs are running for real.

Just as I'm about to push him off the anti-bed, I hear this *whooo-whooo* sound. I think it's probably an owl, since going *whooo-whooo* is what owls are famous for. However, I don't want to take any chances. Believe me, in the dark Woods, I feel a whole lot better keeping my arm around my Loyal Dog, even if he hasn't had much practice fighting wild animals.

So I don't sleep. That's kind of a problem, because as you know, the worst thing about not sleeping isn't being tired. The worst thing is the worrying.

I'm not worrying about starvation. Those yummy Double Stuf Oreos are still hanging from the roof. I'm not worrying about how much Mom is worrying about me. She doesn't even know I'm gone. She thinks I'm sleeping in a cider mill. (Which proves how little she cares about me!) I'm not even worrying about Alison that much. She's got doctors and nurses and Mrs. T. and Lucy all taking care of her. Everybody always says she's got the *good* kind of cancer, so she's going to be fine. Her hair will grow back.

But I am worrying a little about Lucy being mad at me. Lucy hardly ever gets mad, so I don't have much experience with that. And then as I lie there in the dark

Woods on my anti-bed, I remember another time when Lucy and I had a fight.

It was last November, right after the Halloween when we wore different kinds of costumes for the first time ever and Patricia Palombo made Lucy walk with her. I wanted Lucy to come over after school. In fifth grade, we spent almost every afternoon together. But once middle school started, Lucy said she was too busy. I kind of understood that. We did have more homework. And since her mom was tired all the time, Lucy had to do lots of chores like she was a farm girl or something. I guess I should tell you that Lucy's parents are divorced and her dad lives in a foreign country so he is never around. Anyway, I asked her and asked her until finally she came home with me after school.

We did our homework. We ate a snack. And then we just sat there.

"What do you want to do?" I said.

"I don't know. What do you want to do?"

I didn't understand. Lucy and I NEVER had trouble figuring out how to have fun. We always just had fun. I hoped it wasn't because we were sixth graders. "Do you think we're so old that we can't have fun anymore?"

Lucy sighed.

Then I thought, Oh no, we ARE old. Lucy was just sitting at the kitchen table with her head in her hands.

Then suddenly she sat straight up. Her eyes flashed

like the good old Lucy. She said, "I know what to do! I can be Joan of Arc!"

When we were younger, we always used to act out stories. Once we got to middle school, I figured we were too old for make-believe. But I was so relieved that we were going to DO something that I said, "Great."

Lucy had been reading this book about Joan of Arc, so she got to be Joan because she knew all about it. She said I could be the King of France. I agreed, since I didn't have a clue about who he was. But then she started explaining how he was a big crybaby. And the whole point of the story was that I had to be a total loser so she could save me.

I didn't like that. In the past, we had been equal partners in the adventures. So I said, "Maybe I could be somebody else and we could save the King together?"

"No. It's really important that *I* be the one who does the saving."

She was so determined that I said, "Okay."

But being a whining loser was boring. So when she acted out how those dead saints told her to save me, I said, "If you hear voices, maybe you should go see a shrink."

Then she said, "Watch it or I won't save you."

"I don't need to be saved," I said.

"Yes you do. I have to practice."

Of course, NOW I know why she said that. NOW I know why she thought she needed to practice saving people. But back then, all I knew was that I didn't like how she was talking to me, so I said, "Can't we play something without any whining losers?"

Then she said, "You shouldn't complain about my idea since you never have any ideas AT ALL!"

So I shut up. I clenched my teeth so tight they started to grow together. I squeezed them even tighter because my lips were wobbling. There was a little leaking from somewhere near my eyeballs, so I squeezed my eyelids shut too. But I couldn't do anything about my ears.

By the way, someone should redesign people's ears because there's no way to shut them. I don't think I could ever SEE anything that was as awful as HEARING Lucy say I never had any ideas at all.

Then it got worse, because Lucy said, "Now you're getting upset."

Well, wouldn't you get upset if your best friend said horrible things about you?

But Lucy wasn't sympathetic. Lucy, who was usually the nicest, most caring best friend in the whole world, said, "You see? You are just as whiny as the King of France. Only I can't worry about saving you. I can't save everybody!"

"I didn't ASK you to save me. I didn't WANT you to save me. That was my whole point. But you weren't listening to me. You're just being SELFISH!"

She looked at me like I hit her. Then she grabbed her books and went home.

The next morning, I was still mad. By lunch, I was ready

to forgive her. But she sat next to Patricia Palombo instead of me. So I got mad at her again and didn't even wait for her after school. And so it went. For a hundred years.

Two days later, Mom finally noticed how upset I was. She tried to make me feel better. But obviously she hadn't noticed that I wasn't five years old anymore. Having a snuggle and tickling me with the tail of my orange tiger did NOT help at all. I didn't even feel like drawing one of The Best of All Possible Worlds. Those were pictures we made of places we wanted to be. But I didn't want to pretend anything with her. I wanted my best friend. So Mom suggested I call Lucy.

Only that was the problem. "I CAN'T call Lucy!" I yelled at Mom.

Then Mom started her speech about HORMONES and EMOTIONS and how easy it is for girls my age to get overwhelmed by their feelings. As if being my age was a crime or something.

I went in my room and slammed the door.

I heard Mom call Lucy's mom. They had a long conversation. Then Mom hung up and I didn't hear anything for a while.

Finally Mom knocked on my door and came in. She sat down on my bed like we were going to have one of those talks. I was really worried that Mom was going to yell at me for calling Lucy selfish. But she didn't. She gave me a big hug. And then she said Alison had cancer.

Lucy didn't want to talk about it, but Alison wanted me to know so I would understand what was going on.

I guess I nodded like I understood because I didn't want to look stupid. Only I should have asked Mom questions, because I didn't understand.

I still don't. To tell you the truth, cancer totally confuses me. After all, Ginia's birth sign is Cancer the crab (which is totally appropriate). Back before all this happened, Lucy and I laughed about that every time we read Ginia's horoscope in the *Daily News*. What's going to happen to the Crab today? we would say. Obviously Alison didn't have that astrology kind of cancer. But even the cancer sickness was different for whoever had it. When Grandpa had cancer, everybody made jokes like, Don't sit on Grandpa's lap because it's radioactive. No one ever explained where the cancer was. They said I was too young to know about stuff like that. For a change, I was actually glad to be too young, because I didn't want to know about it. It seemed so totally gross. After a while Grandpa got better and I could sit on his lap again. So I figured that would happen to Alison. Still, I knew Lucy had to be worried.

The next day, I tried to give Lucy a hug. But she said, "Don't feel sorry for me."

Then I didn't know how to feel. Because I did feel sorry for her. It must be awful to have your mom have cancer. Even if her lap wasn't radioactive, there were probably lots of reasons you couldn't sit on it. Like once you're in middle school, you're not supposed to need to do that anymore.

Then Lucy said, "Did you do the math?"

And I nodded.

After that, we both pretended like nothing had happened. Like we had never argued. Which seemed like the right thing to do at the time.

Only while I'm lying here on the anti-bed, I remember that I never really told Lucy I was sorry for calling her selfish.

So that means that maybe Lucy never forgave me for that either.

The dark is a misty gray now. I guess the sun's getting ready to come up. I'm hoping that it'll be easier to sleep when it's daylight.

Then I hear a noise I haven't ever heard before.

Outside the shelter, something is snuffling and rustling in the dead leaves.

It's probably Arp. Sure, my good old Loyal Dog must have gone outside to pee. The reason the noise is so much bigger than a little dog is because all noises sound bigger when you're lying by yourself in a shelter with only two walls to keep out what's in the Woods.

Then I hear a little growl right by my feet.

It's Arp, getting all tense and bristly. So he isn't the one outside. And obviously I'm not imagining the sounds, because he hears them too.

Arp barks. I grab him and hold his mouth shut. I hope

if we're really quiet, whatever is snuffling and rustling will just snuffle and rustle right past us.

The sound gets closer and closer until it's a few yards away from the walls. My heart jumps up and down like a person on a trampoline.

There are cracks between the boards. Some are big enough for me to put my finger through. I could lean over and peek at whatever is snuffling and rustling. Do I want to see what's going to eat me? Are you the kind of person who watches the needle get closer and closer when the doctor gives you a shot? Or are you the kind who covers your eyes because what's the point of looking when it's going to happen NO MATTER WHAT?

Well, I don't look. What can I say? I'm a coward. I pull the poncho over my head and scrunch up in a ball with my arms locked around Arp and my knees.

The rustling noise gets closer and closer.

Then something knocks against the side of the shelter with a huge THUMP!

The thump isn't a bump, like an accidental excuse-me bump. The thump has claws that scratch along the wall.

What can it possibly be?

But I still don't peek. I hope that if I don't look at it, then it won't look at me. I know, I know, that's an incredibly stupid hope. But basically that's all the hoping I have left. And anyway, if I see the thing see me, I think I'll die of fright. Maybe you think dying of fright is just an expression. But if you're huddled under a flimsy piece of plastic, and if a THING WITH CLAWS is on the other side of a wall just a few feet from your head, and if your heart isn't even beating anymore, it's just quivering in your chest, then maybe you'll realize that dying of fright is not only possible but probable. The more I think about it, dying from fright is better than getting eaten alive.

I stop thinking all these thoughts when I hear the THING WITH CLAWS walk into the shelter. I guess it finally figured out it didn't need to rip through the walls, since most of those walls are missing.

Arp is really going wild now, but I keep a tight grip on him.

My eyes are still shut tight, but I can't shut my ears or my nose. Now I can actually hear the THING WITH CLAWS breathing. It makes a strange wheezing whistle when the air goes in and out of its nose. And it has a very strong smell. Much worse than wet dog. Plus, it's a bigger smell, so it must be a bigger animal.

The THING WITH CLAWS snuffles around over by the post that holds up the roof. I'm a little puzzled about why it isn't bothering with us, but not too puzzled, because I have very little brain available for wondering about stuff, since it's mostly paralyzed with fright.

Then I hear the THING WITH CLAWS grunt. The grunt noise moves higher. Did it grow taller somehow? Or just stand up?

Then I hear the rustle of plastic. That's right, plastic.

You know that sound. When Mom's driving to the farm-house with me in the backseat next to all the groceries, if I slip my hand into a bag to sneak a cookie, no matter how careful I am, the bag goes *rustle rustle crinkle.* Then Mom says, "Megan, what are you doing?" even though it's obvious because I've been busted by a plastic bag.

Snuffle whistle rustle crinkle.

I don't think there ARE any plastic bags in the shelter.

Then I remember the Oreos. Yes, those dark choco-late cookies double-stuffed with creamy white delicious-ness are in a plastic bag hanging just below the ceiling about six feet away.

I open my eyes to see what's going on with my breakfast.

And there, standing up on its back legs, is a HUGE BLACK BEAR!

It's so tall its nose is as high as the bag. The Bear snuffles the Oreos. Only every time it snuffles, its nose pushes the bag away. The bag swings back and forth while the Bear gets angrier and angrier. I scrunch as far from the Bear as possible, but my back is pretty much against the wall. The Bear shoves the bag around for a while. Then it raises its gigantic paw and swats the bag. Its claws rip through the plastic. And the Oreos fall onto the bed RIGHT NEXT TO ME!

For a moment, I'm frozen there. What if the Bear starts eating Oreos and continues eating me?

I don't have time to worry or be afraid. I pick up the

Oreos and throw them as hard as I can. It's a terrible throw, but at least the package makes it out of the shelter. It lands on the dirt about three feet away.

The Bear drops down onto its four legs. It picks up the package with its teeth. Then it saunters back into the Woods.

When the Bear is gone, I let go of Arp and fall back onto the bed.

Arp immediately starts barking. He's a dog, so I don't exactly know what he's saying, but I guess it's something like "Did you see that thing? Can you believe how big it was? I thought we were goners for sure."

I look up at the shredded plastic bag that still hangs from the post. I don't even mind not getting to eat one single solitary cookie.

All I can say is "Thank goodness for Oreos!"

7
Trail Blaze Betty

I lie there for a long time. I want to let that Bear get a thousand miles away from me before I go back into the Woods.

"Lucy won't believe me when I tell her what happened. Too bad I didn't have a camera to take the Bear's picture."

Arp snuffles the corner where the Bear stood.

"Should we bring that plastic bag to show her how the Bear's claws ripped it to shreds?"

But a torn plastic bag isn't as impressive as an actual Bear.

So I get out the sketchbook and a pencil and start drawing it. As you can see, it isn't easy to draw a bear. The teeth and the claws are very tricky. I put Arp and me in the drawing to show how big it was. Only it's boring to draw us hiding under the poncho. So I draw how we saved ourselves from being eaten alive.

I'm so busy drawing that I don't notice Arp has left until I hear him outside barking. Then I think, Oh no! The Bear came back for seconds.

What should I do? Try to save Arp? Or run the other way as fast as I can?

The yucky voice says, *"You can't save him anyway, so you might as well RUN!"*

I fumble with my shoes. Why did Mom make me wear sneakers that take forever to tie? Arp keeps barking. But it isn't his fierce bark; it's a happy bark. And then I hear someone say, "So you *are* a dog. You're such a little thing, I wasn't sure."

Once my shoes are on, I hurry outside to stick up for Arp. He can't help it if he's a yippy little fluff ball.

An old woman is bending over to scratch Arp's head. Her legs are gnarly and her shorts have too many pockets. She wears one of those goofy round sun hats that are usually white, only hers is orange plaid. But the most important thing to know about her is that she's holding a basket full of little plastic bags. And in each bag is a huge chocolate brownie.

My mouth fills with saliva. I'm not kidding. I have to swallow a bunch of times to keep from slobbering when I say "Hi!" as cheerfully as I can.

She straightens up and squints at me. "I'm Trail Blaze Betty. You've probably heard of me. I'm in all the guidebooks."

I haven't. But that isn't a smart thing to say to someone who's holding a basket of yummy brownies. So instead I say, "Sure, I've heard of brownies. I mean, you."

She chuckles. "That's okay. I know what I'm famous for. Of course, that's just part of what I do. I'm in charge of this whole section. Got to keep the Trail in good shape."

"Sure do," I agree. I figure that listening to her talk for a while is the price I have to pay for a brownie. And if I listen really well, I might get the whole basket.

"Don't find many young people who think that. In fact, don't find any. Most people who care about the Trail are old like me. I hiked the Trail nine times."

"Wow! All the way from Georgia to Maine?"

"That's right." She smiles at me like she's pleased I

89

know that. "Most young people never even heard of the Trail. They don't want to hike anymore. They want to stay indoors in front of their computers. They think a challenge is shooting down imaginary spaceships."

"That's so dumb." I'm not lying. Those computer games are boring. The only one I like is The Sims.

Trail Blaze Betty looks really happy that I agree with her. "You know what the trouble is with people today?"

I shake my head.

"Nobody knows how to survive in the real world. Nobody even spends time in the real world. Everybody zips around in climate-controlled cars. They scream if they see a bug. Or a bear."

"We saw a bear!"

"You saw Matilda? She's such a beggar. Can't leave the brownies in the shelter for the hikers. She just eats them. Or those juvenile delinquents eat them. They like to hang out in my shelter. Didn't build it to be a party place. Built it for the hikers. Like you. And your family."

When she says "family," I know the questions are coming. I better think of a clever lie, because I know people won't think it's a good idea for a kid like me to be hiking alone on the Appalachian Trail. I try to change the subject. "You built the shelter?"

"Sure did. But sometimes I want to tear it down. Makes me so mad to see those young people drinking and carrying on in there. Don't kids know there's better ways to have fun? They think hiking is for old people.

Every year when we have our Appalachian Trail meeting, I tell the other members, 'We've got to get the young people off their butts and on the Trail. It won't matter how many washouts you fix if you can't get the young people to hike.'"

"That's right. Young people should hike." It seems smart to agree with her. But then she squints suspiciously at me from under the brim of that goofy orange plaid hat.

Suddenly I have a horrible thought. If my parents found out I'm not with Ginia, then everybody will be searching for a girl and a little white dog. My picture might even have been on the TV news. But I don't think Trail Blaze Betty has seen me. Anybody who wears shorts like that and hates computer games probably hates TV too.

She shifts the basket from one hand to the other. "So, where is your family? Didn't hear any noise. Didn't know anyone was up here until I saw the dog."

"My family, well . . ."

I haven't thought of my clever lie yet! Now I'm worried. If she thinks I'm not a real hiker, but just a runaway lost girl, will she give me a brownie before she calls the police?

"Are you out here on your own?" she says.

"No. No. My family is up ahead."

"They left you behind?"

"No! I mean, yes. Well, it's hard to explain." I look at

Arp for inspiration. But he's no help. He's lying on the ground right next to Trail Blaze Betty's feet.

Then I notice her shoes are these really old hiking boots. They're so beat-up, they look like she wore them all nine times when she hiked the Trail. So I stop trying to make up a good lie and just start talking. "But you'll understand because you're a hiker. You see, my parents are like you. They think it's really important for kids to hike and do things on their own. Like that boy in the book!"

"What book?"

"It's my dad's favorite. This boy runs away from the city and goes to live in the Woods."

"You mean *My Side of the Mountain*?"

"That's what gave him the idea for me to do it."

"Your parents know you're here?"

"Oh yes." This isn't exactly a lie. They know I'm in the Woods. Somewhere. But she doesn't seem satisfied, so I say, "They're just a mile ahead."

"By the spring?"

For one horrible minute, I'm not sure what kind of spring she's talking about.

"At Elephant Rock," she says.

"Oh. Yes. By the spring at Elephant Rock. They're going to check in with me every mile or so."

"Actually that's two miles ahead."

"Right. Two miles."

"They're two miles ahead?"

"Because they think it's important for me to do it on my own."

"The whole Trail?"

"Oh no! I'm only going to Mount Greylock."

She takes off her hat and scratches her head. Then she puts her hat back on. "Well. You got just a few more days then."

A FEW MORE DAYS! I gulp. But I have to nod like, Sure. A few more days. I knew that.

"Why are you doing this?" she says.

She's really close to me. I can smell those brownies. I can see how her eyes are totally buried in bags and sags. They're sort of cloudy in spots, like how old people's eyes get. She's making me so nervous, I almost make a stupid joke like "To get to the other side." But I don't, because I know whatever I say will be extremely important. So I think for a moment.

"I guess I want to hike the Trail because I can. I mean, I never did anything much. Because I didn't think I could do anything. And that made me feel bad. But then I started hiking and I kept hiking. And now I've made it this far. We even survived the Bear. So I know I can do it. I really can. If I just keep going."

She sighs. She looks even harder at me. Like she can read my brain. Then she rubs her head again and puts her hat on. She points a gnarly finger at me.

"You can do it. But you must respect the Trail. You can lie to your friends and lie to your family and even lie

93

to yourself. But the Trail will find out the truth about you."

I nod.

She nods.

Then we both look down that Trail. It's just a path. It's not like either of us can see anything. But it feels like we're looking into the future.

"Well, I better get going," I say. She doesn't say anything. She's still looking toward Mount Greylock. But I can't wait any longer. I have to ask. "Can I have a brownie?"

She hesitates. Then she holds up the basket.

"Thanks." I try to pick the biggest one. But it doesn't seem nearly big enough, since I'm as hungry as that Bear. "Can I take more than one? For my family?"

"I guess you better."

I cram eight brownies into my backpack. "I have a very big family!" I wonder if I should name them. But I think I'd better leave before she asks me any more questions or changes her mind.

She's kind of in a hurry too. She practically runs (well, I guess it's running for a turtle or an old person) back down the slope, away from the Trail. I wonder how far away her house is. I can't see anything except trees.

"Thank you!" I call after her.

I put on my backpack.

"Come on, Arp."

I head for the next blue splotch.

We walk about half an hour, until I think we're totally out of her sight. Then I gobble up every last one of the eight brownies—even though the lumpy parts aren't chocolate chips but walnuts. I don't mean to eat all eight of them. I'm just so hungry I can't stop. Then I lick my finger to pick up the crumbs stuck to the notes she packed with each brownie.

> Greetings, Hiker!
> Please enjoy these brownies.
> I'm too old to make the trip anymore, but I still remember how much I appreciated the treats people left for me.
> You can do it! The only way to fail is to quit. So keep going! You'll be glad you did. Hiking the Appalachian Trail was the best part of my life.
> Sincerely— Trail Blaze Betty

Now that the brownies are all gone, I feel a little sick and sorry. I read the note again. I remember how she said the Trail would find out my lies. Well, that won't be hard, since there are so many of them. Even Arp, my Loyal Dog, is looking at me with a sorrowful expression.

"What? Brownies aren't good for dogs."

I crumple up the bags and cram them deep in my pack. But I don't want to be reminded of what a pig I was. So I take them out and bury them behind a bush.

"There." I brush the dirt off my hands.

Arp is still looking at me.

"What? For your information, that's where they always put trash. They bury it in a landfill. What do you expect me to do with it? It's not like there's going to be a garbage can around the next corner."

The moment I turn my back, he starts digging up the bags.

"Stop it, Arp. Whose side are you on?"

I carefully cover everything up.

"Weren't you listening when I told Trail Blaze Betty how important it is?"

He looks at me like I must not have been listening either. The brownies have been eaten. So I bribe him with a peanut butter sandwich. Then I remind him, "The only way to fail is to quit, so let's keep going!"

8
Saved!

I don't exactly know how the Trail can find out my secrets, but I don't want to take any chances. For the next hour, I totally respect the Trail. I step over roots. I don't whack trees or kick stones. I don't rip leaves off branches. I try to keep Arp from lifting his leg right by the edge.

"Can't you do that someplace else?" I ask him.

But he doesn't listen. He's having too much fun chasing after chipmunks and rabbits. Sometimes he doesn't even see an animal; he just sniffs along a trail of stink that a wild creature left behind in the dead leaves. He really shouldn't do that. What if the stink trail led to that Bear? Besides, then he always has to run like crazy to catch up.

"Arp, you're wasting energy!"

Does he care? Of course not.

"We have a long way to go. And I'm not carrying you anymore when you get tired."

It's past twelve o'clock. I'm not hungry. Those eight brownies are a big lump in my stomach that won't go away. Like a huge pile of guilt. I'm so hot and tired, all I want to do is lie down and take a nap. But I can't. I have to keep going, because as you might remember, Trail Blaze Betty said that Mount Greylock isn't just around the next bend—it's a FEW DAYS AWAY.

The Trail is in a flat part and not uphill or anything, but my legs just don't want to go. My muscles are saying, Excuse me, didn't we do this yesterday already? How can you possibly expect us to do it again?

I drag my legs along the Trail like they're paralyzed or something. I get another, bigger walking stick. It's too hard to carry, so I drop it. Then I wonder if that's respecting the Trail. Trail Blaze Betty is so crazy, she'd probably want me to put the stick back where I found it.

By one o'clock, I'm sure that Mom and Dad are back from Rutland. Ginia is saying, I thought she went with you. Mom is saying, I thought she was with you. Dad is calling whoever is in charge of finding lost girls. I hope that Ginia is in big trouble. I hope she's sorry she told all those lies. The Trail would find out a lot about her, that's for sure.

Only she's not hiking the Trail. I am. At least, I'm trying to.

Arp and I stop and have a drink. I have to give him some water from the second bottle because there aren't any puddles. Only when I'm giving him the water, he bumps the bottle and the rest of it spills and disappears right into the ground. Of course, when I spill water, it would be someplace where it doesn't even make a puddle for Arp.

I slump down over the empty water bottle. Why did I ever think I could hike all the way to Massachusetts? Who am I kidding? I never did anything my whole life. It's like Trail Blaze Betty said. The Trail will find out the truth about me. And the truth about me is that I'm a lying, lazy quitter.

The yucky voice says, *"You'll never make it, so why even bother to try?"*

And if I'm going to quit anyway, I might as well quit now. Wouldn't that be the sensible thing to do? Wouldn't that save a lot of energy? Because the further I walk now, the further I'll have to walk to get back to Trail Blaze Betty so she can call my parents to come pick me up.

But how can I tell her that I'm not a hiker and the only thing I can do is doodle? What if she asks for the brownies back? Then I'll have to tell her what a pig I was. She seems like the type who gets really mad about stuff like that.

"She told you the Trail would find out your lies," the yucky voice says.

But it wouldn't be a lie if I could just keep hiking. So I stand up. But Mount Greylock seems so far away. Can I do it? No.

I turn around and walk back toward the shelter.

Then I stop. Can I face Trail Blaze Betty? No.

I turn around again and walk toward Mount Greylock. All those miles, all those days. I'll never make it.

I stop. I really don't know what to do. So I say, "I wish Patricia Palombo were here."

Arp looks at me like I'm nuts. He never met her, but he's definitely heard me complain about her.

"If she were, then I'd know I'm doing the right thing, because Patricia Palombo never has doubts about anything. If she's doing it, it's wonderful. If she isn't doing it, it's lame. It's that simple."

I get so agitated, I continue walking again—toward Mount Greylock.

"And sometimes something like lunch clubs switches from lame to wonderful, just because she decides to do it."

Does Arp care? Of course not. He's a dog. He's lucky. He doesn't even know what lunch clubs are. You probably don't either, because everywhere else in the world, sixth graders get to leave school for lunch. But in our middle school, the parents and teachers decided it isn't SAFE to let sixth graders go out, because of this high school right next door. When we complained, the parents and teachers decided to give us lunch clubs for enrichment. As if learning basket weaving or other activities suitable for senior citizens could make up for being deprived of our freedom.

Lunch clubs were voluntary. I mean, they couldn't MAKE kids sign up. So nobody did. Then I noticed there was a club for doing comics. When I was little, Mom and I drew cartoons together. Mega Girl battled Ninja Ginja and saved the world! We did pages and pages. Until Ginia said my characters looked like vegetables and I got mad and quit. But if I drew comics at school, Ginia couldn't make fun of me. So I said, "You know, a club might be okay if it was for something fun like drawing cartoons."

Before Lucy could say what a good idea that was, Patricia Palombo said, "The only enrichment I want is a bigger allowance."

After everybody laughed, I couldn't say any more about it.

A few days later, when I got to the cafeteria, everybody was crowded around the sign-up sheets. First Patricia Palombo put her name down. Then five other girls did. And then Lucy did. I was totally stunned. But she hadn't signed up for the comics club. She signed up for knitting!

I went right over to Lucy. "Why would you sign up for that stupid club?"

Patricia Palombo answered, even though I wasn't talking to her. "Knitting isn't stupid, May-gun."

Patricia Palombo liked to make my name sound dumb when she said it.

She held up a fashion magazine. "Look. Knitting is totally cool. Everybody's doing it."

I turned my back on her to talk to Lucy. "You don't care what everybody's doing, do you, Lucy?"

"I'm sorry, Megan, but my mom needs a hat," Lucy said.

I was getting upset. Since Lucy and I weren't in ANY of the same classes, lunchtime was our only chance to be together. And now she had given up spending time with me just so she could knit. I knew Alison was sick and probably needed a present to cheer her up, but that didn't mean Lucy had to knit a hat. "I'll BUY her one!"

"No. I have to MAKE it for her," Lucy said.

She was being stubborn again, just like when she wanted to practice saving people.

Then Patricia Palombo leaned real close to show Lucy a picture in the magazine. "A hat is such a cool thing to make! Look at how cute they are! We can go to Knitty City by Columbus Avenue to pick out our yarn. Wait till you see the fabulous colors."

So I signed up for knitting too. What else could I do? Of course I was totally terrible at it. My yarn got tangled. I kept dropping stitches. Lucy had to slide them back on my needle. She even offered to finish my rows for me. But I didn't want to be helped like I was a pathetic baby. I wanted to be clicking away like Lucy and Patricia

Palombo, magically turning a long string into a fuzzy shape. So after two Wednesdays, I quit. I couldn't take the humiliation.

Lucy tried to talk me into staying, but Patricia Palombo said, "Why bother? May-gun always quits. Besides, now you'll finally be able to work on your mom's hat."

Needless to say, I HATE Patricia Palombo.

But now I wish she were walking along next to me. Because if she were, then I could shout at her, "Ha-ha, Patricia Palombo! You think you know everything, but you don't. Because look at me. I'm not quitting. I'm hiking the Appalachian Trail!"

I pump my fist in the air.

"No kid in my class ever hiked the Appalachian Trail, I bet. Not even Patricia Palombo. Probably no one in the entire school ever hiked it—including the teachers. But we're doing it, Arp!"

It's like an episode on one of those shows. You know the kind. The main character is this totally cool kid who is an expert world-champion rock climber. And she journeys through the wilderness to save her dad, whose plane crashed on the wrong side of a mountain.

Of course, sometimes in shows like that the main character is a fat, lazy, whiny misfit who must be saved herself. But that's not the situation here. My legs don't feel tired anymore. In fact, they feel totally powerful. I'm not just walking. I'm hiking!

"Hey, Arp! I have an idea. You know how they always do those walkathons for diseases with names you can't pronounce? Well, we're going to do our hike for Alison. Since she can't climb Mount Greylock, we will. We'll call it the Hodgkin's Hike."

I start going faster and faster.

"Maybe it takes Trail Blaze Betty a few days to get to Mount Greylock because she's got old legs. But we'll get there quicker—especially if we keep going like this."

Then I hear a roaring sound off in the distance. I stop, because it isn't like any of the other noises in the Woods.

"Do you hear that, Arp?"

He does. We both look all around, but we can't see anything except the dirt path and the usual hundred million trees. The roaring gets louder and my heart throbs right along with it. "What is it?"

I guess because of my recent experience with Matilda the Bear, I'm worried it might be another wild beast. Only the sound is coming from above my head. Could it be a monstrous vulture? Finally I realize it's a helicopter. But what's a helicopter doing in the Woods?

"Are they reporting on a traffic jam on the Appalachian Trail? Seven-squirrel pileup by Elephant Rock."

Arp looks at me. He's not laughing. Well, okay, he never laughs. But he knows that we shouldn't be joking about the helicopter.

"You think they're looking for us?"

I pick Arp up and bury my face in his fur. Suddenly I want to cry. Why does the helicopter have to come now? I mean, my hiking was going so well. I was even feeling good about myself for a change.

"It's that noise. It's so loud that it's making me upset."

Arp licks my face. That's why my cheeks are wet. And maybe one or two tears.

The roaring is extremely loud now. The whirring blades have stirred me up inside. All my bad thoughts come back to the surface. I remember how scared I was about being lost and seeing the Bear.

"We can go home," I whisper to Arp. "If we want to."

But I don't climb up on that big pile of boulders to make it easier for the helicopter to see me. Instead, I carry Arp into a cluster of bushy trees.

"If we get rescued now, no one will ever believe we were going to make it all the way to Mount Greylock."

I duck down under some very low, scratchy branches and hold Arp tight.

"But we're going to make it, aren't we?"

His tail thumps against my ribs.

"We can't quit now. Remember what Trail Blaze Betty said. The only way to fail is to quit. And I'm tired of quitting and failing, aren't you?"

The roaring gets so loud that the vibrations rattle my body. Arp is whining. But it doesn't matter. Nobody could have heard him. I don't dare look up. It seems like the helicopter hovers right over us for a very long time. I feel like I'm in this weird horror movie where gigantic insects hunt little human beings.

Just when I can't take any more and I'm going to run out of my hiding place screaming, "I give up! I surrender!" the roaring moves on. It gets quieter and quieter, until it fades in the distance.

Now it's just me and Arp, all alone in the wilderness again.

I put Arp back on the Trail. If he could talk, would he say, "I can't believe you turned down a ride in a helicopter!"

I can't believe it either. And now that Mom and Dad have sent a helicopter, I know how worried they must be about me. I really don't like to think about that.

"Well, I could call them if they had given me my own cell phone," I say.

Arp barks. I guess he's had enough of my excuses.

"So what should I do then?"

Arp scratches his ear with his back foot.

"If I go back to tell Trail Blaze Betty that I need to call my parents, she'll know I lied and she won't let me keep hiking."

The only thing I can do is leave Mom and Dad a note. So I rip a page out from my sketchbook. On one side, I put their names and our Vermont address. On the other side I write:

Dear Mom and Dad,

Then I stop. I don't know what to say. The main thing is I want them to know I'm not in trouble. So I just draw a picture of Arp and me, hiking. I make sure to put big smiles on our faces so they'll know we're all right. But Arp looks a little snarly like that, so I try to show his tail wagging. Then I sign it at the bottom.

Your daughter Megan,
who isn't wasting her life,
quitting, or lying around
anymore!

Unfortunately I don't think we'll be passing a mailbox anytime soon. The best I can do is put the note next to the Trail. I stack a few little rocks on the corners so it won't blow away.

"Someone will find it and send it to them."

I rearrange my sock inside my shoe so it won't rub so much. I put on my backpack. Arp dashes off ahead of me on the Trail. His tail is wagging, just like in the picture. He looks so happy that I don't tell him what I'm thinking. Now that we passed up a chance to be rescued, we better make it to Mount Greylock.

9
Dorks!

We hike about a hundred miles through the same old green trees. Or at least that's how it seems. So we're shocked when we get to some enormous gray rocks. They're so huge that they block the Trail.

"Now what?" I ask Arp.

Arp barks at them.

"What are you doing that for? Yapping won't make them move."

Then I remember what Trail Blaze Betty said. "Hey, Arp! One of those big rocks must be Elephant Rock. That means the spring is nearby."

That's good news. It's two o'clock—the hottest time of the day. I haven't had any water since I spilled the rest of the second bottle hours ago. I start searching all around the rocks. But let me tell you, it's hard to look for something when you don't know exactly what it is. It's kind of like that algebra stuff we're going to learn in seventh grade. How can you find what X is when no-body knows what X is? Now I know that a spring is where water comes up out of the ground. But I can't picture how that water would come up. Would there be a pipe and a faucet?

"You'd think they could put up a sign."

Then I notice a blue splotch up on top of the first rock. "Look! That means we climb that way." I feel very clever for having figured that out. Only Arp doesn't want to stay on the Trail. He'd rather go around the rocks, chasing another chipmunk that he's never going to catch.

"Arp! You're going to get us lost."

Does he care? No. I should just let him go, but I doubt he could find his way back, since I don't think he understands about the paint splotches. So I follow him around the enormous gray rocks.

I can't see the chipmunk or Arp. And since I'm a human, I'm no good at following their smells. I'm just about to call him again when I hear laughing from further around the pile of rocks.

"What's that pile of fluff?"

"Hey, Joey. That looks like your mom's wig."

"Shut up!"

"You shut up!"

"No, you shut up!"

Believe me, I don't like hearing those teenage voices. As you probably remember, the last time I encountered

Native Vermont Teenagers, I ended up with green slime in my hair. But then Arp starts barking, so I know I have to do something.

I follow the sound until I get to a place that's kind of like a room made out of rocks. There are five teenagers—two couples who are lying around on each other and one guy who is teasing Arp with a stick.

"You leave him alone," I say.

They all turn to look at me: Stick Guy, Trucker Cap, Blondie, Boston Red Sox Shirt, and Big Pink-Striped Butt.

Big Pink-Striped Butt says, "Oooh, Joey. Better do what she says. She looks mean."

"And crazy," Blondie says.

"She's a wild girl," Trucker Cap says.

I smooth down my hair. I guess I probably do look a little wild.

"She probably bites," Big Pink-Striped Butt says.

Boston Red Sox Shirt jumps up and dances around snarling and Big Pink-Striped Butt pretends to be scared.

Then Arp barks. And Big Pink-Striped Butt pretends to be scared of him too. Only Arp doesn't know she's teasing him. He barks and growls. That makes everybody laugh even harder. I get really angry. I mean, it's one thing for them to humiliate me. But they shouldn't pick on a little dog.

"Stop making fun of him!" I shout.

"Should we make fun of you?" Trucker Cap says.

I'm thinking of all these great things to say, like JUST TRY IT! Or maybe YOU WOULDN'T DARE!

Then Big Pink-Striped Butt looks right at me and says, "I know you."

"Did you meet her in the psych ward?" Blondie says.

"No! She's that girl who got lost in the Woods," Big Pink-Striped Butt says.

"No I'm not!" I say.

"What girl?" Boston Red Sox Shirt says.

"It was all over the news this morning. This girl got lost in the Woods."

"I didn't get lost," I say.

"They said she has a little white dog just like that one. They showed her picture on TV and everything. It's definitely her. Only in the picture she had really weird hair. Part of it was all frizzed out. And part of it was twisted in these bumps," she says.

I hide my face in my hands. That was my sixth-grade picture. It was a complete disaster because Ginia talked me into doing something SPECIAL with my hair. I should've known better than to trust Ginia. I'm sure she deliberately made me look ridiculous. By the time I looked in the mirror, it was too late to do anything except go to school with a brown paper bag over my head. I can't believe that's the picture they put on TV! Why couldn't Mom give them a good picture? Like that one where Lucy and I are sitting on the statue of that dog in

Central Park. I always look better in pictures with Lucy because we're laughing and I'm happy.

Of course, there aren't any happy pictures of us in sixth grade. Mom probably thought that one in the park was out of date. But still, she didn't have to humiliate me by sending out that awful school picture. Now everybody will think that Megan Knotts is a lost wimp with bumpy, frizzy hair!

"Is there a reward?" Joey says.

"There is NOT a reward because I'm NOT lost!" I say.

Then I whistle to Arp and start walking away.

"If you're not lost, then what are you doing all by yourself in the Woods?" Blondie says.

"I'm hiking," I say.

"She's hiking," Blondie says in a singsong way.

"Who'd want to do something like that?" Big Pink-Striped Butt says.

"Joey would. Joey just loves to go off in the Woods and play with his little furry animal friends," Boston Red Sox Shirt says.

Then Joey jumps on him and he punches Joey and Joey grabs him and Big Pink-Striped Butt starts hitting Joey with sissy hands.

I don't wait to see what happens next. I grab Arp and run around the rocks. I know the Trail is somewhere toward the right. But the rocks are too steep to climb back to it, so I just keep going straight ahead through the Woods. I pass a blanket spread out on the ground. At first

113

I think, Ew, gross me out, a love nest. But then I think, Whoa, a blanket! I put Arp down so I can gather it up, and this paper bag that's lying on top of it. Then I really run.

The mound of huge rocks gets smaller and smaller. I hope that when I can finally turn right, I'll cross the Trail. And you know what? I do! There's the wide path with the blue splotches on the trees. I'm so relieved to be back on the Trail. But even though I'm seriously gasping for breath, I keep on running. I need to get far away from those teenagers—especially since I'm borrowing their blanket.

We come to the biggest gray rock of all. It's separate from the others. I don't pay any attention to why it's off on its own—like it ran away too, maybe. But Arp stops right in its shadow and laps at a puddle.

"This is no time to get a drink."

Arp doesn't listen. His pink tongue goes in and out so fast, I can hardly see it.

"Come on, Arp." I'm really mad that I have to pick him up again, especially since he's all wet.

Then I realize—he's drinking. He found the spring!

I pet him and hug him for being such a smart Loyal Dog. But he's too thirsty to appreciate compliments. I'm thirsty too. So I get both water bottles and fill them. I take a nice long drink. The water is so cool and refreshing; it actually tastes sweet. I just finish filling the bottle up again when I hear someone shout.

"HEY, WILD GIRL! GIVE ME BACK MY CIGA-RETTES!"

10
Smoking

"I DIDN'T TAKE YOUR CIGARETTES!"

Don't worry, I don't actually yell that—I only want to. Instead, I quickly crawl into some bushes and lie down behind a log to hide. That log is rotten and full of bugs, but I don't dare move, even after some uncomfortable dampness seeps into my shorts.

The bushes are thick and the voices are pretty far away. Since they're such Dorks, I hope they can't see me through the leaves. But my shirt is yellow (even though it's dirty from being on the Trail). My backpack is hot pink and their blanket is a hideous red and orange plaid. All the green and brown leaves are totally defeated by those brighter colors. Why didn't I get that boring brown backpack Mom liked because it had lots of practical pockets and was on sale? I decide to do a better job of hiding, so I cover myself up with dead leaves.

Unfortunately Arp digs up my legs as fast I bury them.

"Stop it," I hiss at him. "You're not being very loyal."

He whimpers and lies down. The next clump of leaves I pick up is gross and wet with actual worms crawling all in it. When those slimy worms touch my leg, it takes every ounce of my strength not to SCREAM.

Meanwhile, the Dorks crash around, calling, "Wild Girl" and "Lost Girl." Then, as they get madder, they change "Lost Girl" to "Loser," which I really don't like. Sometimes they say, "Give us back those cigarettes, or we'll smoke you!"

I know they can't actually smoke me. But they're getting very angry.

I don't know what to do.

Now would be a good time for the helicopter to come back. Or maybe those little woodland creatures—you know, the chipmunks and rabbits—could all come together to defend me just like I defended them by not letting Arp catch any of them. Or maybe I should just give back the cigarettes and say it was all a big mistake. I only took their stuff by accident because their blanket looked exactly like a blanket I once had. Or something like that. Then, after I apologize, they'll let me get back to my hiking. No harm done, right?

The voices get closer and closer. I grab Arp so he won't bark at them.

Then I hear somebody shout, "What do you kids think you're doing?"

It's Trail Blaze Betty!

There's silence. Then there's a sniggery laugh.

"You won't be laughing when I call the State Patrol," she says.

"What for?" Joey says.

"I warned you if I EVER caught you good-for-nothing kids messing around on my property again, I'd call the State Patrol," Trail Blaze Betty says.

"But we're miles away from your stupid shelter," Blondie says.

"This is my property. The entire Appalachian Trail belongs to the hikers. And I am a hiker," Trail Blaze Betty says.

"We aren't messing around. We're chasing a thief," Joey says.

"This runaway girl stole our stuff. We're only trying to get it back," Boston Red Sox Shirt says.

"You should be yelling at her, not us," Trucker Cap says.

There's another silence. And I think, Uh-oh. What if she listens to them?

Then Trail Blaze Betty says, "Don't tell me who to yell at. I yell at anybody I want. Especially people who throw trash everywhere and don't respect the Trail or themselves."

I'm glad she's mad at them. Then I start wondering if she's also mad at me. Why else would she be here? Did she watch the TV news and find out that my parents didn't say I could hike the Trail? I slither down deeper in the slime and the gooshy leaves.

"Now go on home!" Trail Blaze Betty says.

"What about my cigarettes?" Joey says.

"You kids shouldn't be smoking," Trail Blaze Betty says.

"We aren't. We're just bringing them to Joey's mom," Blondie says.

"I'm sick of your lies. Now git! DON'T MAKE ME TELL YOU AGAIN!" Trail Blaze Betty shouts.

They mumble and grumble, but they leave.

I stay hidden long after their voices fade. The Dorks are gone, but I'm just as afraid of Trail Blaze Betty. She's probably sick of my lies too. After all, I lied about my family and I ate all eight brownies and littered. The Trail found out the truth about me and told her. She probably even knows how I almost killed a Hundred-Year-Old Maple.

"Girl? You there, Girl?" she says.

I'm afraid to breathe.

"You find the spring, Girl?"

I hold Arp's mouth shut.

"Okay, Girl. You got to do what you got to do," she says.

I have no idea what that means. But I'm scared to ask her.

I hear her go along the Trail, back toward her place.

She whistles "Home on the Range" as she walks. Or maybe it's "The Star-Spangled Banner." I can't tell; she's such a terrible whistler.

I wait a little bit longer. When I can't hear her anymore, I let go of Arp. While he rolls around in the dirt, I get up from my hiding place and sit on a rock.

I'm a mess. Slimy leaves are stuck to my legs. I peel them off. The mud is still there. I just sit there, staring at my filthy legs. I probably should go back to the spring and get water to clean them, but I don't. Everything seems stupid. Especially hiking. I mean, I know I shouldn't pay any attention to what those Dorks said. But they weren't exactly impressed by what I'm doing.

I unwrap the blanket and peek inside the paper bag. There's a half-empty bag of potato chips. I give a few to Arp, but I don't even feel like eating them. At the bottom of the paper bag is the pack of cigarettes. I pick it up and rub my thumb along the sharp edge of the box. Then I open the box and rub my thumb over the tops of the cigarettes. There are seven of them. A book of matches is stuck inside the box. I take it out. There are sixteen matches. After I light one of the matches, there are fifteen left. And after I take a cigarette out of the pack and light it with the burning match, there are six left.

Lucy would HATE what I'm doing. After Alison got cancer, we despised the smokers we saw on the street. They should have been going to doctors and having horrible treatments that made their hair fall out. But they

119

weren't. They were walking around puffing on their cig-arettes, polluting the air.

But Lucy won't know if I'm smoking. Lucy isn't here. Lucy didn't come with me this summer. Maybe Ginia is right. Maybe Lucy thinks I'm a whining loser and she doesn't care what I do anymore.

I get so depressed that I actually take a puff. Then I nearly die.

Here's something you probably don't know if you're a kid like me. Cigarettes taste bad. I don't mean a little bad, like a marshmallow that fell off your stick and into the ashes (which you eat anyway because it was the last one in the package). Cigarettes taste so bad there's no way to describe it. It isn't like a flavor. It isn't even a taste. It's a bad-tasting feeling. I have no idea why peo-ple smoke. Except that maybe cigarettes taste so awful that people have to feel better when they stop.

Only that doesn't work. Even after I take the ciga-rette out of my mouth, Arp has wolfed down the rest of the potato chips, my hike is still stupid, and Lucy still doesn't care about me.

So I just sit there, watching the glowing red-hot part of the cigarette creep closer and closer to my fingers. Pretty soon, I can feel its heat. That makes me nervous about getting burnt, so I accidentally drop it on the dead leaves. I quickly jump up to stomp it out before it starts a whole big forest fire.

Then I jump up and down saying, "Fire! Fire! Fire!"

Not because there is one or anything, but because there could be one. In other words, I can MAKE A FIRE!

When he sees me get excited, Arp barks. We both jump around until we fall down exhausted. I give Arp a big hug.

"Isn't it great, Arp? We have a blanket and matches. We don't need to worry about finding another shelter. We can make a real campsite wherever we want."

I cram the blanket in my pack. I put the precious matches in my pocket and we start off again.

"The ideal campsite should be by a little babbling brook and kind of in the open but still surrounded by nice trees. It should be on a hill with a view of a valley. And flowers nearby. And campers that were there before should have accidentally left a big picnic basket full of sandwiches and cookies. Oh, and dog food."

When he hears "dog food," Arp barks and looks up at me like, "Where is it?"

"No, Arp. We don't have any. I'm just hoping that we'll find some dog food."

Arp barks again.

"What are you complaining for? You ate all the potato chips. You shouldn't want any dog food."

Arp barks again.

I sigh. Talking to a dog can be challenging, no matter how loyal he is. "Never mind. Let's go find our campsite."

We walk and walk. We walk through the late

afternoon when the flies are bad. We walk in the early evening when the mosquitoes are bad. (Isn't it nice how they take turns annoying me?) We don't find the ideal campsite. In fact, we don't find a campsite that has even one of the requirements. But we're getting tired and hungry. When the DARK creeps out from the trees again, I get nervous. Sometimes you can't wait for the ideal place. Sometimes you just have to make the best of what you've got.

I stop where a dead tree stretches out of the Woods across a grassy place. "What about this spot, Arp? Hey, maybe that tree could be a bench for me to sit on!"

Arp doesn't say what he thinks of my idea in actual words. He trots right over and pees on the tree. Luckily it's a very long tree, so that wet spot doesn't have to be part of the bench. I go off in the bushes. I'm getting better at finding bathrooms now. I've learned to avoid places with lots of sharp branches.

We're both starving but I decide to make a fire before we eat. Maybe the peanut butter sandwiches will taste better toasted.

I find three short logs and stack them like logs always are in pictures of fireplaces.

"Stand back, Loyal Dog, and watch me make a fire!"

He doesn't move. But I figure when the big burst of flames leaps up into the sky, he'll get his little butt to safety.

I light a match and hold it next to the logs. The match

burns down near to my fingers, so I drop it on the logs. The match burns a little longer and then it goes out.

"Maybe the wind blew it out?"

Arp wags his tail.

"Stop that! You're making a breeze."

I light another match and hold it near the logs. Then I light another. And another. Nothing's happening.

"I don't get it. I have matches and wood. So why can't I make a fire?"

I'm hearing that yucky voice again. *"After all that boasting about making a fire, you can't do it, can you?"*

The sun is setting. The DARK will come. That's practically the only thing I can be certain about—that the Earth will keep turning on its axis. The Earth won't wait until the fire is a cheerful blaze. The Earth will just spin us right into the pitch-black night.

I light another match. It burns out. Now there are only ten left.

"Who cares about a fire anyway? It's not like we have hot dogs to cook."

I throw the matches at my pack. I kick the biggest log. Then I sit down on it and put my head in my hands.

Here's the thing. Say you have a terrible day at school and you come home and slam the door and sit on your bed and sulk. Well, so what? Nothing bad will happen. Eventually your mom will call to you and make you eat your dinner.

But if I sulk out here in the Woods, then Arp and I

will have a long, cold, dark, miserable night. So even though I don't feel like doing anything, I have to try again.

It's getting cold, so I put on the sweatshirt. Then I see that book. Since it's about a boy surviving in the wilderness, maybe it has some good advice for me.

I skim the first chapter. It tells how he has a house in a tree and a deerskin blanket and even a fireplace in there, so he's snug and warm in a snowstorm. But it doesn't explain HOW he made the fire. I flip around and read other parts. Mostly he just blabs on and on about his rabbit-fur underwear and gives recipes for making soup out of turtles and jack-in-the-pulpit roots, like he's some old lady.

Well, I don't have rabbit-fur underwear or a fireplace in a tree. And I don't know what jack-in-the-pulpits are.

Then the yucky voice says, *"You see? He knows how to survive in the Woods. But you don't. So you'll never make it."*

The book makes me so angry that I throw it into the bushes where I went to the bathroom. But I don't care. I'm not going to get it. It's useless.

"Dad, why did you want me to read about that boy?"

I start getting a different kind of upset, just thinking about my dad. He made a fire in the farmhouse fireplace every rainy night. And since it rained practically all the time, that means he made at least twenty fires.

"How come you never watched him and learned how to do it, Arp?"

Arp wags his tail and makes his wrinkle-nose smile, like he's saying, "Because I'm a dog."

Arp is right, of course. He's a dog and I'm a girl. I should have paid attention to my dad. But I didn't. Now I start missing him something awful. I miss his goofy smile and the way his glasses always fall into his dinner plate and how proud he is of his Vermont beard. I wish he WERE here to give me a lecture about something. I would listen—especially if it was about how to make a fire.

Then I remember. I'm so excited, I tell Arp.

"Remember the night Dad asked Ginia to bring in the firewood? And she carried in three smooth, round logs? Dad asked her why she picked those. She said she didn't want to scratch her arms on the rough, splintery ones. Then Dad had her try to light the fire. Only it wouldn't burn. Remember?"

Arp wags his tail.

"Then Dad told her to go back and get kindling. She said, 'Do I have to? Can't Megan do it?'"

I don't want to remind Arp of what I said, because it wasn't very nice. Those days I was very grumpy about Lucy not being there. Anyway, that doesn't matter now. The point is that Dad brought in kindling and split logs. He put most of it on the side and carefully laid a few little sticks in the fireplace. Then he said, "Remember what a fire is. A fire is combustion that happens in oxygen. Where is oxygen? In the air. If you try to burn a thick log, not enough oxygen can get to the place of combustion."

Then, since he is my dad, he blabbed on and on about how Rome wasn't built in a day. The Sistine Chapel took years to build and even more years to paint. Naturally I thought he was nuts. What did the Sistine Chapel have to do with making a fire? But now I understand. You don't build a fire by piling on huge logs. You do it one twig at a time.

"One twig at a time, Arp. Go get us some little sticks."

Maybe you think dogs are experts at fetching sticks. But Arp only picks up the sticks I find for him. And then he gets them all slobbery and wet, which makes them TOTALLY useless.

So I have to gather all the wood. Then I crumple up the brown paper bag. I light a match and light the paper. That makes a nice little flame. But I don't stop to admire it. I feed the flame little sticks, like it's a baby learning how to eat. And you know what? IT WORKS!

Then I'm so totally psyched because I DID IT!

I REALLY DID! ALL BY MYSELF WITHOUT HELP FROM ANYBODY!

After a few more minutes of piling on bigger and bigger sticks, I've made a huge blaze. That three feet of flickering orange heat and light will definitely scare away the bears. And it completely destroys that pack of evil cigarettes. I don't even mind the stink; I'm just glad they're gone. Now Lucy can't be mad at me for having them.

My fire is absolutely beautiful. Now I can toast the last

two peanut butter sandwiches. I stick the bread on long thin sticks. Arp isn't too happy about the burnt crusts, so I give him the nuts from the trail mix and a carrot. We drink some water. Then I wrap myself up in my blanket and Arp jumps up into my lap. We watch the flames wave as they stand up against the dark sky. I tell you, it's just like TV. No, better than TV. Because I made it myself.

I draw a picture of the flames dancing along the logs. But that seems too ordinary for how amazing I feel, so I add a few other things. Because if I can make something warm and light out of a bunch of dead sticks, then I really can do anything.

11
Starving to Death

When I wake up the next morning, the fire is out.

I poke around in the ashes with a stick. They look exactly the way I feel. Cold and gray. They look so pathetic I want to light the fire again. But I don't. I only have nine matches left. Besides, what good will a fire do? Even if I get one started (which is doubtful, because for some reason everything is all wet), I don't think I'd feel as wonderful as I did last night. I'd still be hungry—and lonely.

I haven't seen my family in two days and two really long nights.

It's breakfast time. I wonder what they're doing. Is Dad looking for his glasses? Does anybody tell him they're on top of his head and laugh when he puts them on upside down? Is Ginia using the side of the toaster for a mirror? Does anybody tease her so she'll stop being so vain? Is Mom making oatmeal? Does anybody tell her to stop talking about the different kinds of perspective and stir so it won't burn on the bottom again? Are there four blue bowls on the table? Or did Mom only put out three?

I hope someone gave them the note I left for them along the Trail. They must have been really surprised to see that picture I drew of Arp and me hiking. I hope they know we're absolutely fine—except for being hungry.

Arp comes over, wagging his tail like he's glad to see me. Only I know that to him, I'm not a unique human being with special ideas and powerful feelings. To him, I'm a food dispenser. Or I'm supposed to be.

This is the food we have left: two carrots, a package of slimy tofu, a bag of mushed grapes, two granola bars, and the weird bits of dried fruit from the trail mix. I refuse to count the potato chip crumbs that cling to the empty bag—that would be totally depressing. I give us each a carrot and a granola bar. Arp gobbles his up quickly. That reminds me of Ginia's fast-food diet. She believed that if she ate fattening food fast enough, it couldn't stick to her thighs.

But dogs aren't supposed to be on diets. After Arp eats, he looks at me and wags his tail. He cocks his head to one side. His ears perk up. He puts his paw on my knee. He's so cute. Or he would be cute if I could walk over to the cupboard and get him a dog biscuit.

"Sorry, Arp. But this is my breakfast. You had yours already."

He cocks his head the other way and barks while I eat my carrot and my granola bar. It isn't a vicious bark.

Still I wonder what he would do if he got really, truly hungry. After all, he's an animal that used to be a wolf.

"We better get going."

I don't even want to think about how many more miles to Mount Greylock and how many steps my poor aching legs have to take before we get there. I put my shoes back on my aching feet. Now I have a hole in my sock. When did that happen? I try to rearrange it so the hole isn't right over the sore spot. But this is hard because the hole is the REASON there's a sore spot. I stuff the blanket in my backpack. I make sure the matches are in my pocket. Then I get back on the Trail.

"We'll find more food. Look at all the food we found so far. Maybe brownies and potato chips aren't very healthy, but they ARE food. We won't starve. Soon we'll be in Massachusetts with Lucy."

Arp actually sighs like he's wondering how soon that will be. Since I can't answer that, I keep talking about Mrs. T.

"Mrs. T. isn't the cookie-baking type of grandma. But she loves to eat, so there will be food. There must be Chinese takeout in Massachusetts. Don't you worry."

Only Arp isn't the one who's worried. After all, he's a dog. He doesn't have a yucky voice in his head.

"What about water? You only have one and a half bottles left. What if you go crazy from thirst and drink from a puddle and get poisoned by frog pee?"

We walk and walk. Birds are singing. Little drops of

water decorate the spiderwebs that hang across the Trail. A soft gray mist fills in the gaps between the trees. When the sun gets high enough to peep through the leaves, it makes rays of pure gold. I'm trying to ignore the yucky voice and enjoy the scenery.

If Mom were walking with me, she would say, "Oh, Megan, isn't it magical? Just like an enchanted forest!" If Dad were here, he'd tell me the reason for the little drops of water. If Ginia were here, she'd tease me about my frizzy hair. But since I'm walking by myself with a dog who isn't very good at conversation, I can't think about anything except food.

"Hey, Arp! Look how loose my shorts are! Isn't this a great diet we're on?"

He doesn't say anything. He won't even look when I lift up my shirt to show him the space between my skin and the waistband.

By ten o'clock, the mist and golden rays are gone and the magical forest is the same old Woods. By noon, the walls of my stomach are rubbing against each other. By one o'clock, the acid in my stomach that's supposed to digest food is trying to digest my stomach. I'm so hungry; I don't think I've EVER been this hungry in my whole life.

And then I remember when I was.

Last December—right at the time of year when everywhere you go there's a plate of yummy cookies or a pile of chocolates wrapped in shiny colored paper—Lucy decided to stop eating.

We were sitting together at lunch. I watched her stare at her sandwich. But I thought she was tired of peanut butter, so I offered her the leg of my gingerbread man.

She shook her head. "I can't eat," she said.

"Why not?" I said.

She wouldn't tell me, so I worried about it for the rest of the afternoon. Once we got to sixth grade, certain girls started paying a lot of attention to their bodies. Patricia Palombo was always asking questions like "How much do you weigh?" If you made the mistake of sitting next to her at lunch, she always told you how many carbs were in that mouthful you just swallowed. If you said, "Ask me if I care," she said, "Obviously you DON'T care, May-gun. But you should."

Well, I didn't. Let's face it—I was never going to be the gorgeous type, so why should I go to a lot of trouble? Besides, I didn't have to care how I looked because Lucy didn't care about stuff like that either. At least, the old Lucy didn't.

Only the next day, Lucy didn't eat her sandwich again. She just drank her milk.

When I asked her what was wrong, she said, "Nothing. But maybe you shouldn't come over to bake cookies today."

That made me panic. Lucy was too sensible to starve herself to death like those crazy teenage girls who think it's attractive when your bones stick out. So why couldn't we make cookies? Baking was one of the best things we did together. Lucy would pretend to be a crazy chef like on TV. I made up fake commercials for things like "Butt-Err—the yellow stuff it's a mistake to eat."

Since I still liked food, she might not want to be my friend anymore. So I asked her, "Do you mean I shouldn't come over or do you mean we shouldn't bake cookies?"

"I guess it's okay if you come over."

She didn't sound very sure, but I went anyway. I wanted to show her we could have fun even if we weren't eating. She didn't have to hang out with other non-eating knitters, like Patricia Palombo. (But I brought a snack with me, just in case I needed it.)

We sat at the kitchen table, doing homework. That's the way Lucy was about stuff. She always did all her work first. After I finished my math, I could tell she was stuck on a problem, so I said, "Want some help?"

"No. I can do it."

"It'll be faster."

"I don't care." She bent over the page. Only she wasn't doing the problems. She was just sitting there, looking all sad and tired. I hated seeing her like that. But what could I do? She said she didn't want my help.

Meanwhile, I was getting hungry. I turned away from her, opened my bag of Doritos, and snuck one into my mouth.

"Could you please eat your Doritos in the hall? They're making me nauseous."

Then (I am embarrassed to say) I yelled at her. "Well, your not-eating is making me sick!"

Her face got all red and trembling. She said, "You don't know what sick is!"

Then Alison called from the back of the apartment. "Lucy?"

I hadn't realized Alison was home.

Lucy's face instantly changed, like a switch was flipped. She hurried toward the bedroom. "Coming, Mom."

I followed along too. I wanted to see Alison. We always traded dumb bunny jokes and I knew a good one. I was going to ask her which side of a bunny has the most fur. (The outside!)

Then I saw Lucy tiptoe into her mom's bedroom, and I remembered. How could I be such an idiot? The only reason Alison would be home was if she was sick. And if she was sick, then she probably didn't feel like laughing at dumb bunny jokes. Or did she? I didn't know what to do. I kind of stood by the doorway. I could just barely see the end of the bed. The covers were rumpled. Lucy fixed them.

"Where's Megan?" Alison said.

So then I had to go in. But I was really scared. I mean, I know that cancer isn't contagious or anything. I wasn't scared of that. I was scared of doing the wrong thing, like I always do.

Alison was lying in bed. I recognized the purple-striped cap Lucy made in knitting club. But that was the only way I knew her. Her beautiful long red hair was gone. Her skin was yellow. Her eyes were sunk in dark circles. She looked so awful; I didn't know what to say.

"Megan." Alison held out her hand.

But I didn't go hug her. Her arm was all bandaged and it had purple bruises on it. I just sort of waved. "Hello."

"I'm so glad you could come over. Lucy needs to see her friends," Alison said.

"I'm fine, Mom. Don't worry about me," Lucy said.

"What were you girls talking about?" Alison said.

Oh no, I thought. I was sure Lucy would complain about me, and Alison wouldn't like me anymore.

But Lucy said, "We were just playing. You know, like we always do? Our characters were arguing about the best way to defeat the Evil Sorceress Doritas."

Lucy sat down on the bed and held her mom's hand. I wanted to sit with them, but I didn't know if I should. I would probably bump Alison and make her feel worse.

"Um, I just remembered. I have to do a little more math. Bye, Alison."

I made a dumb little wave and tiptoed back to the kitchen.

The bag of Doritos was still sitting on the kitchen table. Looking at them made me nauseous too. I mean, why are they that color? Does anybody even know? I crushed them into the tiniest of crumbs and turned the faucet on full blast to wash them down the kitchen sink and through the pipes way out into the Atlantic Ocean. Then I crumpled the bag and pushed it under the other trash that was in the garbage can. Then I washed the orange powder off my fingers. Then I took a wet paper towel and wiped the orange powder off the table. While I was getting another paper towel to dry the table, Lucy came back.

She sat down. She traced her finger through the wet part on the table. I was thinking of what to say. Why is it that when you desperately need some really good words, the only things in your brain are Styrofoam peanuts?

Finally Lucy said, "My mom has been having chemo."

I nodded.

Lucy kept rubbing the wet part of the table long after it was dry.

Suddenly I had a news flash. "Is that why you're not eating?"

Lucy nodded. "Mom can't eat anything. The drugs they gave her don't help. The chemo still makes her throw up."

"But it's supposed to make her better."

"It's a poison, Megan. It makes her better by poisoning the cancer and her stomach."

"And her hair." I started to cry.

Lucy shushed me. "She'll hear you. She hates people feeling sorry for her."

So I hugged Lucy because I wanted her to hug me. "Why didn't you tell me?"

"You know how you get, Megan."

Actually I did not know HOW I GET. In fact, I remember getting a little mad that she would say that. But I was also wishing there was something I could do to help her help Alison. So I said, "I won't eat anything either until your mom can."

"Oh, Megan." Lucy hugged me tighter.

I kept that promise. I had thrown away the Doritos. At dinner, I pretended I had an upset stomach. (Actually that wasn't hard, since Mom had made beans and rice AGAIN, like she always does when she's too busy painting to go to the store.) Skipping breakfast was harder to get away with. But I kept Mom from noticing my bowl was full of oatmeal by asking her if art should be mandatory in public schools. By lunchtime, I was STARVING TO DEATH. I'm not kidding. I almost fainted on the way to the cafeteria.

I felt so noble and loyal, not eating anything with Lucy. We each sipped our milk. Then she left to go to the bathroom and I was there all by myself. I looked in the brown paper bag just to see what Mom had packed for me. Not that I was going to eat it or anything. After all, I had promised Lucy. Luckily it was a disgusting egg-salad sandwich on whole wheat bread, so I wasn't even tempted. I picked a little at the crunchy stuff on the crust that normally I would never ever eat. And that's when I decided that eating food I didn't like didn't really count as eating, since the main idea was to suffer like Alison. If I ate egg salad with those mysterious pieces of green stuff, boy would I be suffering. So I gobbled up every last bit of it.

When Lucy came back, I saw her stare at my crumpled-up paper bag.

"Lucy, I had an idea. You know how we aren't eating because of your mom?"

Lucy sighed.

"Well, if the point is to suffer like your mom . . ."

"Never mind, Megan. I know you ate your sandwich."

"Only because it tasted so awful that eating it made me feel even more terrible than not eating it."

"Stop making excuses. I knew you'd never do it."

Then she left before I could ask her HOW she knew I'd never do it. I mean, I hadn't planned to eat my sandwich. I had planned NOT to eat my sandwich. So how could she know what I was going to do?

Besides, that very day Alison got furious with Lucy for not eating. Lucy had to have extra vegetables and protein to make up for the meals she had skipped. A few days later, Alison was able to eat bananas, soup, and other yellow foods. And when Alison had more chemo right after Christmas, Mrs. T. came to make sure Lucy ate.

But I didn't say "I told you so," like I could have.

Even though I was right, I know I was wrong too. I didn't tell Lucy she should eat because she couldn't help her mom if she got sick. No, I just made a mess of it by pretending and lying and quitting.

"Just like you always do," my good old yucky voice says.

My foot is really killing me now, so I stop walking. I take off my shoe. I dump out some dirt. Then I drink some water and eat the dried fruit from the trail mix. It tastes better than it looks. Unfortunately it only makes me hungrier. Like that little bit of food woke up a sleeping monster—my stomach.

The only thing to do is keep going. I try to fix my sock again. But the hole gets so big my toes won't stay in. The sock is useless. Just like me. I groan.

Arp looks at me like "What's up?"

I don't want to tell him how I let Lucy down. He'll lose confidence in me. Then he'll start wondering whether we're walking all these zillions of miles and starving and getting eaten alive by bugs to see someone who might not be glad to see us. Who actually has a few reasons to be mad at me.

I go into a frenzy of bug-swatting. Arp barks at me like I'm playing. Only I'm not playing; I'm going insane!

It's so unfair. Especially the part about being starving and getting eaten at the same time. I mean, what's up with that?

Then I freeze. "Be quiet, Arp," I say.

In the distance, I can hear someone whistling that goofy Star-Spangled Home on the Range song.

Oh no! Not Trail Blaze Betty!

12
The Lake

Why is Trail Blaze Betty still following us? Doesn't she have anything better to do? Why doesn't she go back and put the other two walls on that shelter?

By the time I get my shoe on, the whistling is very close.

"We can't get ahead of her now. We better hide until she goes past."

I drag Arp off the Trail and into some bushes.

This is a big mistake. The bushes have prickly thorns that attack me. But I keep going. I can't even cry out because I'm afraid Trail Blaze Betty will hear me. I'm in total agony when I hear the sound of girls laughing.

I stop. But they aren't laughing at me—even though I know I look completely ridiculous stumbling through the bushes silently going *ow ow ow*. They're laughing because they're happy.

Then I hear water splashing.

141

"Come on, Arp. I bet those girls are in a swimming pool."

I fight my way through all kinds of scrubby trees and vines until finally I see the water.

You probably already know there aren't any swimming pools in the Woods. It's a little lake. But from a distance, the water is a beautiful blue. So Arp and I keep going toward it until I can see the girls dancing around on the far shore.

One girl's swimsuit has magenta bottoms and a lime green top. The other girl has lime green bottoms and a magenta top. It's like they're such good friends that they traded. They drag a little yellow raft into the lake and paddle around. The magenta-top girl tries to tip it over. The green-top girl is squealing, but I know she isn't scared—she's just having a wonderful time.

They're having the summer that Lucy and I were supposed to have. The summer of s'mores and wishing on falling stars and laughter and more laughter. The summer of no past and no future, no homework to do and no one to bother us, just best friends having an endless sleepover.

But Lucy didn't come.

The two girls lie on the raft and drift around. They don't paddle to get anywhere. They don't need to. They're together. That's all that matters.

It's not fair that they're floating so free and easy

while I'm scrambling through the bushes. I mean, why couldn't one of their moms have gotten sick? Why does it have to be Lucy who is worried to death? Only Lucy would never say "worried to death." She never lets anybody say things like "I was so embarrassed, I could have DIED." Or "That homework nearly KILLED me." Or even "You make me SICK."

Lucy is such a good person and Alison is such a nice mom. But Alison got cancer anyway, so Lucy got worried. And (even though I'm not as nice as they are) I got worried about Alison too, no matter how many times they said she had the *good* cancer. How can cancer be good? But I couldn't ask anybody that. I couldn't talk about any of my feelings. Not even to Lucy.

When I get to the lake, the water that looked so beautifully blue turns out to be muddy and gunky and choked with weeds and infested with slime-loving creatures JUST LIKE ALL THE OTHER STUPID LAKES IN VERMONT.

I hate Vermont. I really do.

Please don't be like my dad and tell me how the blue water is only reflecting the sky or whatever it does. I don't want to hear anything logical. I just want Lucy and me to be those girls floating on a yellow raft.

Arp happily wades right into the water and has a nice drink. He doesn't know about disappointment and sorrow. He's just a dumb dog. He doesn't even have any friends, unless you count the cat that sleeps in the dry cleaner's window and hisses at him whenever he trots past.

The girls stop playing with the raft and drag it onto the shore. Magenta Top spreads out towels. Green Top gets two bottles of purple Vitaminwater and a bag that looks like lunch out of a little cooler. I'm hoping it's such a huge lunch that there's plenty to share. But I'm worried because there are TWO girls. And when you're talking about hanging around with friends, THREE is an unlucky number.

Still, I walk along the shore closer to them. After I go a little ways, I have to walk in the water because there are bushes in the way. Arp swims along with me. I think he has his eye on the lunch too.

Unfortunately the lunch is just two sandwiches. Even if you cut each one in half, it still wouldn't divide up for three. It's an impossible mathematical problem.

Green Top has hair just like Lucy's. Dark and straight and never completely staying in a ponytail no matter how many times she smooths it back. Of course, the girl isn't Lucy. Lucy doesn't even have a swimming suit like that.

I'm anxious to see the second girl's face. I mean, I know it isn't me. OBVIOUSLY. But if it's someone LIKE me, then it'll be a sign. I never used to pay attention to signs until last year, when Lucy started picking up pennies for good luck. Actually, until last year, I never needed signs of good luck because I always had Lucy. But now I'm desperate for some good news, no matter where it comes from. So I'm hoping hoping hoping as I wade past the bushes and get out of the lake to walk on the pebbly shore.

Suddenly I hear dogs barking way off in the distance. It isn't Arp. He's still swimming in the water. It's a lot of dogs and they sound big. They sound so big that Arp gets out of the lake to be close to me.

The girls hear the barking too. As they stand up and look toward the sound, they notice Arp and me. Their eyes get wide when they recognize us. Then I realize what the dogs are for—sniffing us out.

I pick up Arp so we can run away really fast. But it's too late for that.

"Wait!" the Lucy girl says. "You're Megan, aren't you?"

"And that's your dog, Arf?" says the other girl, who (I have to say) has smooth yellow hair and looks much more like Patricia Palombo than like me.

"Arp," I say.

"Wow!" the Lucy girl says. "Everybody's been looking for you. They say you ran away."

"I thought you were kidnapped or maybe even dead," the blond girl says.

"I'm not," I say.

"What are you doing in the Woods?" the Lucy girl says.

I don't have much time to explain. The barking is still pretty far away, but it's getting closer. "I need your help."

"What for?" the blond girl says.

"You see, I was supposed to be having this wonderful summer in Vermont with my best friend. But her mom is sick. So she decided to stay with her mom even though she would rather have been having fun with me. She is very unselfish that way."

"Oh," the Lucy girl says, very sympathetically.

"So?" the blond girl says.

"So since my best friend couldn't be with me, I decided to go on a journey to be with her," I say.

"Why didn't you just drive?" the blond girl says.

Why didn't I?

"Because." I pause. The barking is making it hard to think. "I can't drive."

The blond girl smirks. "Obviously. But your mother could."

"No. Nobody can drive you when you're going on a journey like this. When you're making a quest to prove your friendship, you have to make sacrifices or the journey won't mean anything. You have to endure hardships. You have to be brave. You have to go on a Hodgkin's Hike."

"What's a Hodgkin's Hike?" the blond girl says.

"It's when you refuse to quit in spite of all the obstacles," I say.

146

"Wow," the Lucy girl says.

"So will you help us? The search party will be here soon. But we can't get sent back now. We have to keep going until my friend and I are reunited," I say.

"Of course we'll help you! What should we do?" the Lucy girl says.

"Let me pretend to be one of your friends," I say.

"But you don't have a swimsuit," the blond girl says.

"You can go in the water," the Lucy girl says.

Am I desperate enough to put my whole body in that disgusting water? Luckily I get another idea. "What if I wrap up in your towel?"

The blond girl wrinkles her nose. I guess I'm pretty gross after all that sweaty hiking and three days without a shower.

But the Lucy girl hands me her towel and puts a big floppy sun hat on my head. "Put your backpack by the cooler. Sit down with your knees up. Now drape the towel over your shoulders."

"The dogs will smell her," the blond girl says. "I can smell her."

"We have to keep away from them," the Lucy girl says.

"What if we all get on the raft?" I say.

"There isn't room," the blond girl says.

"Then you can stay on shore," the Lucy girl says.

"Fine then." The blond girl sits down on her towel and folds her arms across her chest.

147

I pick up Arp. The Lucy girl holds the raft steady while we climb on. I drape the towel around my shoulders and cover up Arp. Then the Lucy girl gets on and paddles us out into the middle of the lake.

The barking dogs burst over the hill. Four big German shepherds strain against their long leashes. Two men run with them down to the edge of the water where Arp and I started wading.

"Hey, girls!" a man with a brown beard shouts over the barking.

"Hey!" I try to sound normal, like I talk to men with yelping dogs all the time.

"You know about the runaway girl, right?" Brown Beard says.

"Sure do!" the Lucy girl says.

"Megan." The blond girl says it in a way like she could have been naming the name. Or she could have been calling me out.

"Have you seen any sign of her?" a man with a black beard says.

"Well . . . ," the blond girl says.

I'm so nervous; I squeeze Arp too tight and he whimpers. But he doesn't bark.

"No," the Lucy girl says firmly.

"Are you sure? The dogs were definitely following a scent," Black Beard says.

"We haven't seen anyone all day," I say.

The dogs snuffle around right where Arp and I went

into the water. Their leashes get all tangled up as they try to figure out where to go next.

"What time did you get here?" Brown Beard asks me.

I don't know what to say. I don't know what time it is. What if I say a time that's after the time that it actually is? I move my arm to check my watch. Then the towel slips down off my shoulder. I'm making a mess of everything AGAIN.

But the Lucy girl saves me. She spins the raft so the men can't see me pull the towel back up. "We came here at ten o'clock," she says.

The towel won't stay, so I have to use my chin to hold it. The men are staring at me.

"Ten o'clock?" the blond girl says.

"That's right, because my mother dropped us off on her way to her yoga class, so I'm POSITIVE it was ten," the Lucy girl says, "We've been here this whole time and we haven't seen anyone."

"Could Megan have been here before ten?" Black Beard says.

"Don't see how she could have made it this far at all," Brown Beard says. "We'd better head back toward where she was last seen by those other kids."

"She should have stayed put! People are much harder to find when they wander around," Black Beard says.

"Let's go. Come on, girls!" Brown Beard shouts.

I hold my breath. But he's calling the dogs. They yelp as everybody runs back up the hill.

I shut my eyes. I feel my muscles go limp. But none of us move for at least five more minutes. Then Arp wriggles out from under the towel and jumps around so much he tips the raft. The Lucy girl and Arp topple over into the water. But I hang on for dear life.

"Good thing that didn't happen before," the Lucy girl says as she pulls the raft to shore.

"Hmph," the blond girl says.

I climb off and give the Lucy girl back her towel. She doesn't use it to dry herself; she puts it far away.

"Thank you. You saved our lives," I say. That reminds me that we're dying of something else too. "It's kind of embarrassing to ask you this, but do you have anything we can eat?"

"You can have what's left of my sandwich." The Lucy girl gives it to me.

"Thanks." I put it in my pack.

Then she hands me her bottle of Vitaminwater too. I drink it all right away. I'd forgotten how delicious it is.

"Can we have your autograph?" the Lucy girl says.

"Really?" I can't believe it. Mrs. T. likes to get autographs from Broadway stars. But they're famous actors. I'm just a kid who's going on a hike. I try not to smile, but I'm really happy.

"What you're doing is so amazing!" the Lucy girl says.

I take out my sketchbook and draw a picture of Arp
and us with the raft.

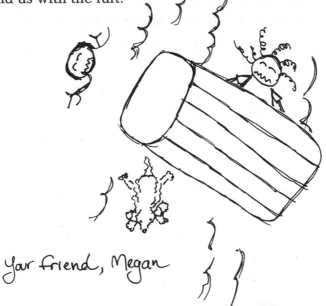

Your friend, Megan

"Huh," the blond girl says. "My mom says you're
just a juvenile delinquent who ran away to be with her
boyfriend."

"My boyfriend? Geez. I won't even be twelve until
next month," I say. Lucy will die laughing when she
hears I have an imaginary boyfriend.

"I'm glad you told us about your Hodgkin's Hike,"
the Lucy girl says. "I knew you had a good reason for
running away."

"So people are pretty worried?" I say.

"Of course they are," the Lucy girl says.

I don't like to think about that. "Didn't they find the
note I left on the Trail?"

"Yes, but they're still worried," the Lucy girl says.

They probably don't believe I can take care of myself. But I can—at least until I get to Mount Greylock.

It's hard to finish the drawing because I have to keep wiping my eyes. I wish I could explain everything to my parents. After I'm done, I say, "You think if I gave you a letter, you could mail it for me?"

"Mail it?" the blond girl says like that'll take forever.

"I mean, e-mail," I say.

I write my mom's e-mail address on another piece of paper. Then I stop writing. I still don't know what to say.

Don't worry. Really, I'm fine. I'll see you soon. Maybe in a day or two. Arp says hello. You were right about a lot of things! And I know

I would write more, but a horn honks. I jump.

"Don't worry. It's just my mom," the Lucy girl says as she takes the papers.

A mom-sounding voice calls, "Amelia! Lindsey! Time to go!"

"Coming!" the Lucy girl says.

"Will she come down here?" I whisper.

"Not if we hurry," the Lucy girl says.

"But I can't find my flip-flops," the blond girl says.

"They're right by the path. Come on. Hurry." The Lucy girl grabs the raft, the cooler, and the towels.

"Thanks for saving us," I whisper.

"Good luck," the Lucy girl whispers back.

They disappear up the path. I hear the blond girl say, "Do you still want to watch that movie?"

The Lucy girl says, "Of course I do. Mom, can Lindsey come over?"

I don't hear the answer. Their voices are swallowed by the Woods.

Those friends are still together. But Arp and I are all alone.

We share the sandwich fifty-fifty. He gobbles his part, but I try to eat slowly. It's chicken on brown bread that is very bumpy with whole grains. I don't take off the lettuce and tomato or wipe off the strange green spread. I guess good old mayonnaise isn't allowed in Vermont. But believe me, I'm not complaining. It's the best sandwich I've ever eaten.

After I lick my fingers and chase down every last crumb, I stare at the two smushed rectangles in the grass where the girls lay on their towels.

"I meant what I said, Arp. We are on a quest to prove our friendship. We have to keep going until Lucy and I are reunited and I've proved to her that I won't let her down anymore."

Arp isn't listening. He's rolling in the dirt. So I put my

hand on his belly to stop him because I need someone to pay attention to what I'm saying.

"They won't say that I'm a quitter after I've hiked all the way to the top of Mount Greylock. Right, Arp?"

He smiles. Although maybe he isn't agreeing; maybe he's just enjoying how I'm scratching his belly.

Then the yucky voice points out a huge problem. *"Lucy doesn't know you aren't a quitter anymore. Lucy is probably busy knitting Halloween costumes for her and Patricia Palombo."*

But she will know! When I get there. So it's back to the Trail again.

13
Off the Trail

Remember all those troubles I had getting to the little lake? Remember the bushes with their prickly thorns? Well, guess what? To get back to the Trail, I have to go through them all again. Only this time, I'm going UP-HILL. Now it's about two-thirty in the afternoon. The sun is blazing on my head. I get so hot that I'm almost tempted to go back to the lake. But even if I wanted to jump in that water, I couldn't.

"Remember, Arp, we're doing something so amazing that the Lucy girl wanted our autograph."

Then just when we're almost back to the Trail, I see something orange. It's Trail Blaze Betty's hat. THEN I remember why we left the Trail in the first place. We had to get away from her.

I grab Arp to keep him quiet and back a little ways down the hill.

The orange splotch isn't moving. I hear a weird

spluttering sound. Is she snoring? Since she's an old person, she might be taking a nap. Maybe if we hike way around her, we can get ahead of her again before she wakes up.

So that's what we do.

Unfortunately this kind of hiking isn't easy. Arp doesn't care that we're battling the Woods. He scoots under bushes. He's SHORT! He isn't getting scratched. He has FUR! He isn't worried about being caught. He's a DOG! But I'm really struggling. Each time I get poked or scratched or whacked by skinny little branches, it seems I'm being punished for not being a good enough friend to Lucy.

After about thirty minutes, I think it's safe to go back to the Trail.

Guess what? I hear a helicopter!

I think, Come on, people. Didn't you get my messages? We don't need rescuing.

They probably didn't get the e-mail yet. So we crouch down in the bushes and wait for the helicopter to go away.

That horrible noise makes me feel really anxious. I hold onto Arp really tight. *Thwacka thwacka thwacka.* Why can't they let us finish our hike in peace?

"I know I told those girls that my journey wouldn't mean anything without hardships, but do the hardships have to be so hard?" I whisper to Arp.

Finally the helicopter fades away. Arp and I return to

the Trail. The hiking isn't torture anymore. But as we go along, I don't see any inspirational butterflies. Or springs with delicious, fresh, cool water. Or mountains with stone monuments on top and stores where you can buy Oreos. I just see the dirt under my feet. My shoes are really dusty and muddy now. The rest of me is totally brown too, except for the red scratches on my legs and arms. I don't know if the Trail is finding out my lies, but it sure is taking over my body.

I try to encourage Arp. "Mount Greylock has got to be just past that next hill."

But it isn't.

"Okay. So it must be just past this hill."

But it isn't.

So I stop saying that.

We walk and walk. We drink some water and walk some more.

It's getting close to five o'clock. Soon it will be dinnertime. Only there isn't any dinner. It seems like we ate that half a sandwich three days ago.

Now Arp won't walk, so I have to carry him. He shouldn't be so heavy, since he's such a little dog. But he is.

I wish someone would carry me.

Oh, Lucy, I think.

If only I could call her. She'd say something encouraging. I know she would.

Maybe if I send her a thought, she'll send one back. Amazing things can happen. I mean, I'm climbing these hills even though I'm hungry and tired and carrying a dog. If I can do THAT, then why can't my thoughts whiz to her? Weren't we always thinking the same thing at the same time? Well, maybe not always. Maybe not so much last year. But we used to. Like the time we were meeting at the playground and I forgot to tell her to bring colored chalk but she did anyway.

I shut my eyes and think really hard. (But I open them after I trip over a root.)

Lucy, this is the hardest part. Maybe you think seeing the Bear was worse. Bears are scary and they smell bad. But you don't need a friend to escape from a Bear; you just need some cookies to throw. You do need a friend to keep you going through the tough times. When you're completely worn down.

You've been worn down too. You've been on a long hike with a big hole in your sock. You've been thirsty and tired and hungry. And scared and lonely. And hungry. I guess I said that already. The ground is so hard it feels like it hits you each step you take. The bugs are so bad that you can't ever even stop and rest because they're out to get you.

I don't want to rest anyway. Not until I make it to the top of Mount Greylock. I don't care how much I suffer. I have to finish my Hodgkin's Hike for you and your mom.

I stop walking because my heart's pounding too loud and I want to make sure I can hear her answer.

Lucy. Are you there? Are you listening?

Maybe I should have kept my eyes shut. Maybe we're too far away. Maybe telepathy doesn't work.

"Or maybe she doesn't want to answer," the yucky voice says.

Unfortunately I can hear the yucky voice loud and clear.

But the voice is lying. Lucy would want to answer me. Wouldn't she?

The yucky voice says, *"Why should she help you when you never helped her? In fact, you got mad at her for wanting to be Joan of Arc and called her selfish!"*

The yucky voice is right. I did.

Now, of course, I know that Lucy wasn't being selfish. She was the OPPOSITE of selfish. She wasn't thinking about herself at all. She was just one big ball of worry about her mom.

Now I remember that after I called her selfish, she said, "I thought you were my friend."

Did I say, "Lucy, I am your friend. I'm your friend when it's kindergarten-easy because all you have to worry about is taking turns on the swing. And I'm still your friend, especially now that we're older and everything is more complicated."

Well, what do you think? Did I say that?

No. I said, "I thought you were MY friend."

I sit down on a rock.

Arp comes trotting over. He sits down too and cocks his head at me.

"What?" I say.

Then he barks two short barks. I figure that means food. Basically that's all Arp ever talks about.

"How can you be hungry? We had that nice sandwich."

Arp barks again as if to say, "That was just a half of a half a sandwich. And besides, we ate that hours ago."

I'm thinking the same thing.

But I don't open up my pack. I mean, I know what kind of food is in there.

I just sit there feeling miserable.

Then I remember something Mom always said to me whenever I came home from school upset. It didn't matter if the teachers were awful or if Patricia Palombo made mean comments about my carbs and my clothes or if no one laughed at my jokes. Mom would say, "You're just tired and hungry."

Then I would say, "NO I'M NOT," and slam the door to my room.

Now I realize that Mom's partially right. I AM tired. I AM hungry. That's why my hike isn't going very well anymore. But I can't tell Mom she's right. She isn't here.

Suddenly I miss her so much I almost start crying again. Only I know that would be a total waste of water. So I open my pack. I put on the "I ♥ Vermont" hat because I know Mom would want me to wear it. (Besides, the sun is in my eyes and I'm too tired to turn to face the other way.) Then I get out my sketchbook and I start to draw The Best of All Possible Worlds, like we always used to do. When I was little, we mostly drew circuses, because I always wanted to be in the Greatest Show on Earth. I would be the funniest clown, and Ginia would be a snarling lion in a cage.

But now I draw Mom wearing the Chinese shirt I like that has the big dragon. I draw me sitting next to Mom. I know I should put Dad in there too, but I'm tired of drawing people, so I just draw his glasses. I do draw Arp. But I figure that Ginia's probably off somewhere with her boyfriend, Sam. Then I draw a picnic blanket. I cover the blanket with food. Fried chicken, potato salad, brownies, watermelon. Then I think, Hey, this is a picture. I can have whatever food I want. So I draw banana splits and shrimp cocktail and egg rolls and big tall chocolate milk shakes.

Drawing makes me so hungry that I could eat the paper. But I don't. I get out the lunch bag. "Come on, Arp. Let's have some delicious dinner!"

I say it in a really loud, cheerful voice. But it doesn't help. There are only two things in the bag. A package of white tofu covered in brown slime. And a bag full of what used to be purple grapes but is now pale green scum.

I open the tofu package. I offer to share. Arp doesn't even give it a sniff. He'd rather eat something he finds in the dirt. I don't blame him.

"There are people in the world who like this kind of stuff. I'm not kidding," I say.

After that inspirational thought, I hold my nose, open my mouth, and drop in one of the strips of slimy tofu. It sort of slithers down my throat. Then I eat the rest of the strips and the smushed grapes.

You probably expect me to tell you that they're actually delicious. They aren't.

THEY'RE THE MOST DISGUSTING THINGS I'VE EVER EATEN!

14
Arp!

By the time I recover from eating the tofu, it's after six o'clock. Arp seems to think we should just make a camp where we are. But I want to hike some more. About thirty trees further along the Trail, I can see a lot of huge boulders. I think that if I climb up on them, I can see above the trees. And since mountains are so big, I should be able to see one in the distance, especially one with a tall stone tower on top.

"Then we'll know how close we are," I tell Arp.

When we get to the boulders, they are even bigger than Elephant Rock. But Arp isn't interested. He lies down on a pile of dead leaves and goes right to sleep.

"Wait here for me. Guard my pack, okay?"

He doesn't answer. (But then, he never does.)

So I climb.

The boulders are smooth and pale yellow. At first, I climb ones that are like stair steps. Then I get to one

163

that's as big as a truck. After I walk along the top of the truck, I realize I picked a dead end. There's a huge gap about three feet wide between it and the other boulders. I'm going to have to turn around, go all the way down and climb up a different way. What a total waste of time—and energy.

I look at the gap again. Too bad I can't jump across it. I stick out my arm to measure the distance. Then I realize it only seems far. I take a few steps back to get a good running start. Then I race toward the edge and take a huge leap.

I'm flying through space. It feels so great. Then I realize something else. I didn't hear the yucky you-can't-do-it voice! It didn't tell me that I'll never make it, I'm going to fall, and that's a really deep gap so I'll probably kill myself.

"YAHOOOO!" I shout.

I fly so far that I stumble as I land. My hands scrape on the boulders. But hey, who cares (even though the palms of my hands are probably the ONLY parts of me that aren't already scratched or bit or sore from hiking). The yucky voice is gone!

I feel so good I look for more places to leap across. I don't find any, so I dance around as I climb to the top of the pile. From there, I can see for hundreds of miles. It's like being up on the Empire State Building, only I don't see other skyscrapers; I see the Woods and meadows and lakes and green mountains.

I feel like I'm looking back at my life. That lake way down there could be the lake where the Lucy girl saved us. Those trees and trees and more trees are where I have been walking forever. Way, way off in the distance I can see a barn. I know it isn't our barn—still, I imagine Mom painting it, even though it's almost seven o'clock and *ART* time always ends at noon. If they still have *ART* time. If they haven't been worrying too much about me to paint anything. But by now they should have gotten the e-mail. I hope they did.

I wave my hand even though I know none of them can see me. Then I wave my whole arm so much, I nearly tip over. But they still can't see me.

A gray shadow passes over the barn. Then I feel sadder, even though I know it's just a cloud. From on top of the cliff, I see the different parts of the land change from light into shadow and back into light again. I know, I know, what's the big deal about clouds moving around? But to see it happen is amazing. If I were down there in that dark patch, I'd be grumping. But from up here I know the sunshine will eventually come back, because I can see it. I can see everything.

Except Mount Greylock.

Still, I feel better. The yucky voice is gone! I can't believe it. I know my legs are stronger from all this hiking. But maybe the rest of me got stronger too. Soon I'll apologize to Lucy and everything will be all right again. At least, I hope so.

I take a different way down. Even though I'm proud of my spectacular leap, I don't want to push my luck. My palms really sting now. I need some water.

By the time I get back to the Trail, I'm about twenty trees further along. Maybe my Loyal Dog will bring my backpack to me so I won't have to walk all the way back to it and then all the way here again.

But I don't see Arp. He isn't where I left him.

I run back. Do I have the wrong place? No, there's my backpack. I pick it up and put it on.

"Arp!" I hiss.

I'm afraid to call too loud. Even though I haven't seen anybody in a while, the Woods are so dense you can't really see who might be lurking around trying to rescue us. And you certainly can't see where a dirty little dog went.

"Arp, you picked a terrible time to chase a rabbit. We have to keep going. Mount Greylock is further than I thought."

But I refuse to worry. I just got RID of that yucky voice. No way am I letting it back in my head. After all, Arp is always running after animals and running back when he can't catch them.

I hold my breath to listen. I hear the wind rustling the leaves, the creak of trees, the twitter of some birds, the buzz of a zillion mosquitoes, and the thumping of my heart. But I don't hear that cheerful little jingle of dog tags, or that little yip-yip bark I used to find so annoying.

"Oh, Arp."

I don't have a clue about which way he went. All I can do is wait for him to come back. But I can't sit still. I have to do something. I wander around behind the pile of boulders. Some people left some trash there. I crush a soda can with my foot and pick it up. Maybe getting a few Salvation Points will help me find Arp.

You probably don't know about Salvation Points. I invented them one day last spring after school when Lucy and I were waiting for Mrs. T. Unfortunately we weren't going to the theater; she was taking Lucy to visit Alison in the hospital. But she was late. After we waited for over half an hour, Lucy got so nervous and anxious she started picking up trash.

"Are you trying to get Salvation Points or something?" I said.

"What are those?" She was really interested.

I didn't want to tell her that I was making a joke. (What can I say? MOST of my ideas start out as jokes.) So I said, "They're points you get for doing good deeds."

"Who gives them to you?" she said.

"Nobody. You just get them. And when you have enough, then . . ."

I almost said, "Then your mom will get well." But I was afraid to. What if Alison didn't? If you want to know the truth, I was afraid to mention her mom at all, because whatever I said would be wrong. If I said that everything would be fine, Lucy would say, how did I know? If I said how worried I was, that would just make Lucy feel worse.

Lucy didn't say anything. But she picked up trash faster, like it was a competition. When she had a huge pile of soda cans and ice-cream bar wrappers, Mrs. T. zipped up in a yellow taxi. She was so excited, she was shouting out the window. "Good news, good news. We get to bring your mom home!"

Lucy jumped in the cab with Mrs. T. and they drove off.

I was very glad that Alison was going home. But I have to say, I didn't like being left behind to put Lucy's pile in the garbage can.

There are no garbage cans on the Trail. Whatever I pick up, I have to put in my backpack. I hope I get double Salvation Points for that. There isn't much—just three more soda cans and two Slim Jim wrappers. Unfortunately there's plenty of room in my pack from where the food used to be. I crush the other cans and cram everything in. Then—you won't believe this—as soon as I zip it shut, I hear a little yip.

"Arp? Is that you?"

I hold my breath, hoping to hear it again.

There it is—a bigger little yip.

"Where are you?"

I can't tell. The yip sounds like it's coming from inside the boulders. But that doesn't make sense. So I run down the path. The yip sounds fainter. I run in the other direction. The yip sounds even fainter.

As I run, I can't help noticing that the shadows are starting to creep out from below the trees. DARK is coming.

I know you're thinking, Well, duh. DARK comes every night. Who can forget that? But maybe you did forget that when DARK comes to me, I can't just flip a switch to turn on a light. I can't carry a fire around like it's a flashlight. I have to find Arp fast if I'm ever going to find him. Of course, that kind of thinking does NOT help at all. That kind of thinking is practically BEGGING the yucky voice to whine again.

My brain is totally stuck like someone going around and around in a revolving door. That makes me think that Arp must be stuck too. Or else he'd just come running to me. It's hard to get stuck in the Woods. But it's easy to get stuck in an enormous pile of boulders. Every boulder has a gap between it and the next one. The taller the boulder, the deeper the gap. Since gaps connect to other gaps, a little dog could fall down and down and down until he's under the whole huge pile.

"Where are you, Arp?"

He barks. Too bad I can't tell where the sound is coming from.

Even though my heart's going a mile a minute, I refuse to panic. I'll just look in every single gap until I find him.

I try to be organized about looking, but I keep forgetting if I've checked a place or not. All the boulders are made of the same yellow-white rock. I can't tell them apart. I feel like I'm looking in the same gap over and over and never finding him.

"Where are you, Arp?"

He barely answers. His bark sounds kind of raspy and weak.

Then a frightening thing happens. The entire pile of rocks glows RED.

It's like a horror movie or something. I quickly jump off those evil boulders. Now I don't even want to look at the rocks. Then I realize the red isn't the symbolic blood of Arp or anything like that. It's just the red of the setting sun. That makes me feel a little better, although the sun going down is horrifying enough.

I need to get smarter about this searching. I need to be the girl who leaps across obstacles, not the girl who crashes down in the gap.

Then I think, What if Arp followed me? What if he tried to make that leap and fell? I scramble up the first few boulders and run across the one that's the size of a truck. I look down into what I boldly jumped across.

And there he is!

I'm so glad to see him, I almost start crying. He's so glad to see me, his whole body wriggles. He barks and barks. I lie down on the rock and reach toward him. I stretch my fingers as long as they will go. But it's no use. My hand is nowhere near him.

"Come on, jump up." If he jumps really high and I grab on to his collar, maybe I can pull him up to safety really fast before he chokes to death.

But he doesn't jump.

"Jump, you dumb dog!"

Of course, he doesn't know what I'm talking about.

"Why did you try to leap over this gap in the first place? You should have known you'd never make it!"

He puts his head down on his paws and whines. I'm so sorry I yelled at him. He only tried to follow me. He can't help it if his ideas are bigger than his legs. I lie down on the rock so I can reach toward him again.

I still don't know what to do, but I feel better lying there. The rock is warm. I know that's just because it sat in the sun all day, but it's comforting—like when you put your face against a little dog's furry body.

"Don't worry, Arp. I'll get you out of there."

The only trouble is, I don't know how.

I lie like that until I can't feel my arm anymore. It's a floppy dead fish stitched to my shoulder.

I feel totally terrible. I've done plenty of bad things in my life. I put shampoo in the tip of Ginia's toothpaste tube (but that was on April Fools' Day). I scribbled "THIS STINKS" in the comment book for Patricia Palombo's science-fair project (but only after I heard her say my color wheel was babyish). And I know you remember how I almost killed a Hundred-Year-Old Maple. But getting Arp stuck is the absolute worst thing ever.

Maybe I didn't MAKE Arp fall down into that gap. But I made him come on this hiking trip. Of course, I wouldn't be hiking if it weren't for Ginia. And none of us would be in Vermont if it weren't for my parents. I try to blame them, only I can't. I'm the one who ran away and decided to hike all the way to Mount Greylock. I'm the one who refused to get rescued. Because of me, an innocent little dog is dying of thirst in a crack in the Earth.

I pour a little water down the gap to give him a drink, but he won't tip his head back and open up his mouth to swallow. The water splashes on his head and makes him muddy and the rocks slippery. So I stop.

The shadows keep spreading out from the Woods. There's no way I can rescue Arp before it gets dark. In fact, I don't know how I can rescue Arp at all. The sun coming up in the morning won't change anything— except by then poor Arp will be even weaker and thirstier.

There's only one thing to do. I have to get help for Arp. And the only person I know in the Woods is Trail Blaze Betty.

Of course, Trail Blaze Betty is the LAST person on Earth I want to find. She'll be really mad that I didn't take better care of Arp. She probably likes dogs better than people because dogs never throw trash on the Trail. She might be so furious that she'll take me straight to the

State Patrol. That would be the worst possible end to my trip.

Actually no. The worst possible end would be if Arp never gets out of the hole.

I slowly walk to the gap and peek over the edge. It's getting harder to see him in the dark. But I can tell he isn't so perky anymore. He barely even looks up at me.

"Arp? I have to go get help to get you out of there. I'll be back really soon."

Then I have an even worse thought. What if I can't find Trail Blaze Betty? It's been five hours since I saw her hat. What if that orange splotch wasn't her hat? If she stopped following me, then I'll have to go all the way past the lake, up that path the Lucy girl went on, and onto the road. Then who knows how far I'll have to go to get help. I mean, this is Vermont. It's not like there are cops on every corner.

I don't have time to explain all that to Arp. I just say, "Don't worry, I'm coming back. I swear."

He doesn't look convinced. He looks so sad. His ears sag. Of course, that could be because his fur is still wet from when I poured water on his head. But it looks to me like he's giving up hope.

Then I have an idea. "I'm going to leave my backpack here with you, so you know I'll be back."

I take it off and hold it over the edge, waiting for Arp to move a little so I won't drop it on his head. Then I think, Am I an idiot or what? If I drop my pack down there, how will I ever pull it back up?

And then *bam!* A lightning bolt hits my head and a lightbulb flashes on, like you see in cartoons. I jump up and down and dance all around singing, "I'm a genius. I'm a genius." I'm SO happy!

"Who needs Trail Blaze Betty? Who needs grown-ups? I can rescue my Loyal Dog ALL BY MYSELF!"

But I better hurry because the second I have my brain flash, the sun drops behind the trees. That means I have about an hour of twilight left.

First I dump everything out of my pack. I'm so excited about being a genius and everything that I'm in too big a hurry to be careful—until the tube of sunblock slides off the rock and down into another gap. Good thing I didn't really need it because I'm always in the shady Woods. Then I carry the rest of the stuff over to the ground where it's safe.

Once my backpack is empty, I take the blanket and loop it through the straps. Now the backpack makes a clever little basket and the blanket makes a rope. I scramble back onto the boulder and show it to Arp.

"See what a genius I am? I've invented a Dog Rescue Device. I'll lower it down to you. You get on it, and I'll pull you up. Got that?"

My plan works perfectly. I lower the Dog Rescue Device into the gap. But the looped blanket is only a few feet long. To get the Dog Rescue Device all the way down to Arp, I have to kneel on the rock and reach down with my arm.

Plop! The Dog Rescue Device kind of lands on Arp. But that's okay because now I have his attention.

"Come on, boy. Get on so I can pull you up."

He doesn't get on. He just stands there, with his tongue lolling out.

"Arp! I can't pull you up if you don't get on the back-pack!"

My arm's turning into that dead fish again. I'm afraid I'll lose my grip on the blanket. "Please, Arp, get on. I can't hold it much longer."

I'm getting so frustrated. I want to scream, "YOU STUPID DOG!" But I remind myself to stay calm. It isn't his fault. He's just a dog. He doesn't speak English very well. He doesn't know what I'm trying to do. He doesn't care about anything except food. Of course! FOOD!

I pull up the Dog Rescue Device and run over to where I dumped out everything that was in it. There must be something to eat. Don't I have any dog food? Carrots? Trail Blaze Betty's brownies? Barbecue potato chips? Is everything gone? Even the slimy tofu? Didn't I save anything? I'm the stupid one.

I'm so mad at myself, I throw one of the cans that I picked up. Salvation Points are useless! *Bam.* It crashes into a tree. *Bam, bam, bam.* I throw all the cans. Then I try to throw the Slim Jim wrapper, but the plastic clings to my fingers even when I shake my hand. I'm desperate to get rid of it, since it really stinks. What's in a Slim Jim anyway? I give it another sniff, just like a dog would.

JUST LIKE A DOG WOULD?

"Arp! I know what to do!" I fold up the wrapper to keep the smell trapped inside and then I scramble back up the boulder.

I carefully fasten the Slim Jim wrapper to the Dog Rescue Device with my lip-gloss key chain. Plastic isn't food, but if it smells like food, Arp will go over and sniff.

I slowly lower the Dog Rescue Device. *Plop.* It hits the ground. Arp walks over. At first I worry, What if he just stands next to the Dog Rescue Device and sniffs?

But he doesn't. He looks at the wrapper. Then, I swear to you, he looks up at me with his head on one side like "What's up?"

So I explain it again. I speak really slowly and carefully. And I act everything out with one arm as I talk. I probably look like an idiot, but I don't care.

"Arp. Sit on the Dog Rescue Device and I'll pull you up to safety."

And you know what? He does. He gets on the Dog Rescue Device. He snuffles the Slim Jim wrapper. I give the blanket a tug. He staggers a little bit and sits down. But he doesn't jump off. He sits there while I pull and pull.

He's very heavy for a little dog. It's hard to keep a good grip on the blanket. When he's about three feet off the ground, he almost falls off. The rough rock is scraping the skin off my knees. But no matter what, I just keep pulling up the blanket. Hand over hand over hand.

Finally there he is. Safe on top of the rock.

Before he can step off the backpack, I grab him up and hug him. I whisper stuff to him that would be embarrassing to tell you, so I'm not going to. I just hold him tighter and tighter while he licks the tears off my face.

15
Taking the Plunge

After all that, we are so exhausted that we can barely climb down off the rocks to make our camp. I build a little fire to take our minds off being hungry. Then I draw a picture of me saving Arp with the Dog Rescue Device. I want to save the Slim Jim wrapper as proof of my genius, but Arp eats it. What can I say? Sometimes he is such a dog.

And besides, he's hungry.

We both are.

Arp sniffs the backpack. He gets excited and starts scratching at it. At first, I think he's just trying to get the leftover potato chip crumbs. Then I open up a little zipper pocket, and guess what? I find a little bag with two peanut butter cookies. I can't even guess how long they've been there. But it can't be more than a year, since I only got the backpack last September when I started sixth grade.

The cookies are hard as rocks. After a little experimenting, I discover that if you break them into little chunks and put a chunk on your tongue, it kind of melts into something you can eat—after about five minutes.

The cookies save our lives. But they also make us thirsty. I take a sip from the water bottle. I pour some water for Arp on a rock that's kind of shaped like a plate. The last thing we need is for him to look for a puddle and get lost again.

Now we have about a half bottle left.

We don't sleep very well. Being hungry and thirsty are two more reasons to hurry up and get to Mount Greylock, besides finding Lucy and apologizing. I make sure the fire is completely out. We start back on the Trail before the sun comes up.

"This way we won't run into any other people," I tell Arp.

The gray light makes the Woods look different. I was

used to the good old green trees blocking my view of the sky and the brown leaves cluttering up the ground. But in the gray light, there aren't really colors, just ghosts of colors. So I talk to Arp more than usual, to encourage him (and me).

"Remember, there's a store on top of Mount Greylock."

He doesn't respond.

"Maybe you've forgotten what a store is, since we've been in the wilderness for so long, so I'll tell you. A store is a place where you can choose whatever food you want. It has rows and rows of aisles. Each aisle has rows and rows of shelves. On each shelf are rows and rows of packages. And in every single package is food!"

Arp isn't as enthusiastic about this as I am.

"Okay, so maybe you've never been in a store, since most of them say No Dogs Allowed. But stores are really great. And the one on top of Mount Greylock will be the greatest of all, since it's on top of a mountain."

Then he lies down right in the middle of the Trail.

"Don't you believe me?"

He lets out a huge disappointed sigh that sounds much worse than any sigh my parents ever used to try to make me feel guilty.

"Okay, I'll carry you. But only to that tree."

I actually carry him further than that, since it isn't clear which tree I meant. As I walk, I keep on the lookout for food.

Actually everything is food. The leaves are food, if you're a caterpillar. The tree trunks are food, if you're a beaver. The dead leaves are food, if you're a worm. The worms are food, if you're a bird. But dogs and humans are totally out of luck.

"There's got to be something around here we can eat! Why didn't anybody teach me which of those little mushroom thingies is really a yummy delicacy? Why did we waste our time learning long division?"

Now I'm really sorry that I threw away the book my dad gave me. I kind of remember that boy talking about which plants were good to eat—when he wasn't busy bragging about his rabbit-fur underwear.

After the sun rises, the birds get a little quieter. The colors come back to the Woods. Green, brown, green-brown, brown-green. And sometimes there are different colors. Dark green, light brown, dark green-brown, light brown-green. Then suddenly I see red!

I put Arp down and run over to some bushes on the sunny side of the Trail. Red berries are nestled among the leaves. As I reach in to pick one, little thorns scratch my arm. But I don't care. "These are raspberries, right?"

I don't know why I'm asking Arp. He never pays any attention to fruits or vegetables. I hold the berry between my thumb and my forefinger. It has the same bumpy surface as a raspberry. I sniff it. It doesn't smell like Razzle-berry lip gloss. But that's a good sign. Then I look at the bush again.

It's exactly like the one by the farmhouse, where Arp likes to take a dump. Last Friday, Mom made Ginia and me pick raspberries. I only got five, and I refused to eat the one that looked like it had been nibbled by a mouse. But Mom said, "Isn't it wonderful to walk out our door and pick fresh raspberries? Aren't these the best you've ever tasted?"

Mom was wrong. The ones on this bush are the best, most delicious things I've ever tasted. Luckily this bush has hundreds more than what we picked last Friday.

That seems like such a long time ago. But it was only a week, because today is Friday. So that means this is my fourth day on the Trail.

I'm too hungry to think about that for long. After I eat five more handfuls, I pick some for Arp. He refuses to eat them. So I have to put them in his mouth. I tell him, "It's for your own good."

He goes *gack gack gack* for a while, but eventually he swallows them.

After I eat the rest of the berries, we keep walking.

"That was just an appetizer. In a mile or so, we'll find some food you like better."

After a mile or so, we haven't.

"There's got to be something," I tell Arp.

Only there isn't.

As usual, we're surrounded by millions of insects and worms. I know that people in those TV shows have swallowed them. But I'm not that crazy or desperate—yet. So eating little slimy things is out. Birds are impossible to catch. Besides, they don't have enough meat anyway. Rabbits have more meat. But even if Arp could catch one, I don't think I could stand to kill a cute little bunny. What we need to find is something big enough to eat, dumb enough to catch, and ugly enough so that I won't want to keep it as a pet.

I'm just about to ask Arp if he's smelled any animals like that when I hear voices.

"Look!" a woman says.

I scoop up Arp and hide deep in some bushes.

"A tufted titmouse!" the woman says.

"Where?" a man says.

"I don't see it," a kid says.

"In that tree!" the woman says.

I look around as best I can, without leaving our hiding place. Maybe a tufted titmouse is something we can eat.

"Up in that oak?" the man says.

"I still don't see it," the kid says.

"Oh, sorry. It flew away," the woman says.

So a tufted titmouse is a bird?

"I'm hungry," the kid says.

"We just started hiking. We can't have our snack yet," the woman says.

The family keeps walking toward my hiding place. Judging by the whining, the kid's probably about my age. As they get closer, I can see that it's a boy, dragging

183

his feet, just like I would have done. It's hard to believe I was ever like that, but I was—before I started hiking the Trail.

"I want to go home," the boy says.

"Don't you want to see a few more birds?" the dad says.

"I never see anything," the boy says.

"That's not true," the mom says. "You saw the blue jay."

"Who cares? Everybody sees blue jays. I want to see something special," the boy says.

"You will. Just look harder," the dad says.

"No. You always see the best birds because you walk ahead of me. But I'm going to be first." The boy sprints ahead along the Trail.

The parents run after him, shouting, "Stop! Stop!"

They catch him just about twenty trees past my hiding place.

"Don't ever do that again. Do you want to get lost in the Woods like that girl and never see your family again?" the dad says.

"Yes!" the boy says.

I put my hand over my mouth.

"And starve to death and get eaten by a bear?" the mom says.

"Did she really get eaten by a bear?" the boy says.

"Nobody knows what happened to her," the dad says.

Well, I know. But I'm not about to say. Although it

184

makes me mad that they're using me as a warning to keep kids from doing stuff. I don't want to be a cautionary tale. I want to be an INSPIRATION!

"You can be the leader, if you walk," the mom says.

"I won't get lost anyway," the boy says.

"How do you know?" the dad says.

"Because that girl got lost in Vermont. And this is Massachusetts."

MASSACHUSETTS!

Outside, I'm staying absolutely, perfectly still while the bird-watchers continue along the Trail. Inside, I'm jumping up and down and turning cartwheels. (Actually, inside is the only way I can turn cartwheels.)

MASSACHUSETTS!

There wasn't a sign like on the freeway. WELCOME TO MASSACHUSETTS. Or a fat red line across the Trail. There wasn't a river like between New York and New Jersey. There wasn't even a lot of a certain kind of store. Like if you drive into Vermont, then suddenly everywhere you see people selling maple sugar stuff. (I don't even know what Massachusetts is famous for selling, do you?) So who knows when we crossed the border? The important thing is that we made it to Massachusetts.

"It can't be long now," I whisper to Arp.

Arp is having a nap. He doesn't seem to appreciate the good news.

"We're really close to that store where we can get food."

He barely even wags his tail when I talk to him. When the bird-watchers are a long way away, I put him on the Trail and start off. But he won't walk. Not at all.

"Arp, if you don't walk, we can't get to the food."

He whines a little.

"I can't carry you the whole way."

Then I hear more people coming. Massachusetts is a lot more crowded than Vermont. I pick up Arp and leave the Trail to go deeper into the Woods.

After about a hundred yards, we come to a little stream. I let Arp have a good long drink. That makes him feel better. He snuffles under some soggy rotten leaves, but he doesn't find anything to eat.

I sit on a rock and splash water on my arms. I don't dare drink it, but it sure feels cool on all my itchy insect bites.

Then I see some teensy little minnows. They're so small they hardly count as fish. I show them to Arp. "Catch one! You can eat it, if you catch it."

Arp tries. He barks and splashes in the stream. But the minnows are too quick and too little.

"We need bigger fish," I say.

I watch the water rush past. A few sticks float by, but not any bigger fish. "Bigger fish probably need a bigger stream. I bet if we follow this stream, eventually it will join a river, and so on and so on, until it's the Atlantic Ocean."

Arp looks at me.

"Don't worry. We're not going THAT far. We'll just find a river so you can catch a fish."

Arp cocks his head.

"Come on." I start walking along the edge of the stream. I step from rock to rock. Arp stays on the bank, slithering under the bushes. I go faster than he does. Well, my legs are longer. But I can tell he doesn't think much of this plan. To be honest, neither do I.

Let me tell you the whole trouble with the world. You never get to choose between something you want and something you don't want. Your mom never says, "Would you like broccoli or a chocolate-pudding cup?" Your mom says, "Would you like broccoli or cauliflower?"

If we keep going away from the Trail, we might not even find a river. And if we do find a river, Arp might not be able to catch a fish. Even if he catches a fish so we don't starve, we might get lost for real (only no one will be looking for us, since we have told them not to). Then we'll never make it to Mount Greylock. And I won't finish my Hodgkin's Hike or apologize to Lucy so we can be friends like we were before.

But if we stay on the Trail, we won't find anything to eat. Instead, people will find us. And once they find us, our journey won't end in triumph. We'll have suffered all these miles for nothing but failure. All we'll prove is how dumb we were to even try.

Broccoli or cauliflower?

More people pass by along the Trail up above us on the ridge. It's a whole summer camp. "Stay with your buddy. Don't leave the Trail," the counselors shout.

But here's the thing: sometimes if you want to be with your buddy, you have to leave the Trail.

Then I see a place where the stream empties into a river that's definitely big enough for real fish. I run on ahead, happy that at least this much of the plan is going right. I run through what looks like tall grass along the shore. AND SINK IN GUNK!

I stop running and pull up my left foot. I lose my shoe. Then, as I lean over to pick it up, I sink some more and fall *splat* in slimy goosh!

Apparently Vermont isn't the only state with disgusting water.

But I can't worry about that. I have to get my shoe. I can't hike without it. After slipping and sliding in the gunk, I grab it. Then I crawl to a dead tree that stretches across the river like a bridge. I pull myself up on it just as Arp comes trotting down.

"Be careful!" I warn him.

He stays away from the weeds and goes over to a little pool that's a few feet from the river. When he wades in it, the shallow water barely gets his belly wet.

"That's not deep enough for a fish. They're all in the river. Come on, what are you waiting for? Catch us a fish."

As usual he doesn't listen to me.

I dip my shoe in the water to rinse off the mud. Then

I toss it onto a big flat rock on the shore to dry. I throw my other shoe over there too. That rock will be a good place to build a fire to cook the fish. And you better believe I'm going to cook it. Patricia Palombo and her friends always brag about the best place to eat sushi. But they'd scream their heads off if I handed them a real live raw fish.

Arp is still just standing in the little pool. Sometimes he snaps at a dragonfly.

"What are you doing? That's no way to catch a fish."

I can see that I'll have to do something. But what?

The book I threw away probably told exactly how to make a fishing pole out of a tree and carve a fishhook out of another tree and make a fishing line by tying pieces of my hair together. But it's no help to me now.

"I did my job, Arp. I found the river. Now you have to catch the fish."

He just drinks a little water and shakes the drops off his fur.

"You know how much I hate going in the water," I tell him.

Then I look down at the river. I'm thinking, What am I afraid of? I've already survived so many worse things. Then I realize something. I'm not that kid who's scared to death of what's in the water anymore. I'm Nature Girl.

And if I jump in the river from the log, my feet won't sink in that slimy goosh by the shore.

I take off my shorts and my shirt and toss them to dry land. (I keep my underwear on.) I walk out further along

189

the log until I reach the middle of the river. I only hesitate for a second. I mean, if you were standing on a log in your underwear, would you spend a lot of time worrying about what's in the water? Then I jump in.

I don't sink in gunk. I'm swept along by a rushing current!

Somehow, I fight my way to the surface. Once my head is above the water, I try to swim back to the tree bridge. But I can't. The current carries me further and further downstream.

Arp is barking. When I try to call to him, I get a mouthful of water. I'm swept around a bend. The current spins me around. Then I gasp. Up ahead, I see white froth as the water crashes over some rocks. Beyond that, I can't see any more water. The river ends in a waterfall. But does it drop two feet? Or two hundred?

The water rushes on. I bump into rocks below the surface. But I can't hang on to anything. It's all going by too fast.

I try to swim straight to shore, but I can't. The water pushes me toward the falls.

Then I notice a tree growing out of a rock along the shore between me and the end. The rock sticks out into the river. And the tree has a branch that's hanging in the water. I swim as hard as I can sort of with the current, but toward that branch. It looks thin. But that doesn't mean it isn't strong.

When I get to the branch, the current almost sweeps

me past it. I have to reach back to grab it. The branch bends and bends. I think it's going to break! But it doesn't. I just hang on to it for a moment, trying to catch my breath. Then I pull myself along it until I get to the rock. Now the current is pushing me against the rock. But somehow I get one leg up, then the other knee. Finally I'm lying on the rock, with my arms around the tree, splattered by spray from the churning water that rushes past.

I'm shivering with exhaustion and the cold. When I feel brave enough, I stand up. Now I can see over the waterfall. It isn't two hundred feet; it's barely even four. But when I see all the smashed logs at the rocky bottom of the falls, I'm glad I didn't have to go there.

In the distance, I hear Arp bark.

"Stay!" I'm afraid he'll follow me. I quickly slide down off the rock on the side closest to the shore. My feet land in gunk! Beautiful, slimy goosh grabs at my legs and holds my foot. When I get to the edge, I don't go back onto dry land. I wade where the current isn't so strong. The water feels cool and refreshing. It soothes my bug bites. If I weren't so worried about Arp, I'd probably go swimming again.

Here's something you probably already knew about lakes and rivers. It's sort of obvious, but I never realized it until this moment. Lakes have gunky parts you don't even want to think about. But if you stay out of the lake because of them, you'll never find the parts that are good.

I wish I could tell Lucy that. I wish I could tell her

how I know I'm awkward and clueless and no good at knitting, but I also have good parts. I'm a lake. And other people are more like bottles of water. Maybe the bottles have fancy labels, but inside it's just plain water.

I wade up the river, around the bend. Arp is still standing by the little pool, right where I left him. "Arp! Here I am!"

Does he run toward me? Does he leap into my arms and lick my face all over? Is he glad the river didn't sweep me over the waterfall and carry my broken body all the way to the Atlantic Ocean?

No. He isn't. He just barks at that little pool.

I'm so annoyed I stomp over to him. "What kind of Loyal Dog are you?"

But I don't say anything more. Because as soon as I get to the pool, I see what he's barking at. Somehow (and I'll never know how, since I was a little busy when he did it), Arp trapped a big speckled fish!

16
The End?

After I finish congratulating Arp for being such a terrific Loyal Dog, we watch the fish flop around in the little pond.

Yes, it's flopping because it isn't dead. It's very alive and it's trying to flop itself back to the river. But we can't let it swim away.

"Kill it," I say to Arp.

Arp barks. I guess he's saying, "I caught it, so you kill it."

I shut my eyes. I wish I was sitting in a restaurant and watching the waiter put a big plate of fish and chips on the table in front of me. But I'm not. So I open my eyes. I don't wait around for the yucky voice to tell me I can't do something. I find the biggest rock I can hold in one hand. Then I bash the fish on the head.

Now the fish is definitely dead. It looks more like the fish I see in the grocery store. But it's different because I killed it. I carefully put the rock down. Then I say a little thank you to the fish for feeding us. "Don't feel too sad,

Arp. It's all part of the cycle of life. It ate a bunch of little fish and now we eat it."

Arp barks at me. He isn't interested in big questions about life and death. He's saying, "So let's eat it already!"

There's one problem. I don't know what to do next. "There were probably instructions in that book. Why did you let me throw it away?"

Arp barks. I guess he's saying, "Shut up about that book and just clean the fish." So I do. First I get a fire going on the flat rock where my shoes are drying. Then I find the sharpest stone I can. I saw off the fish's head so its eyes can't stare at me anymore. Then I slice open the body and scrape out the disgusting bits. To be honest, it mostly looks disgusting, but I try to keep the parts that remind me of tuna salad. Then I make a kind of grill with a bunch of really green sticks and I lay the fish on it.

Of course, while I am doing all this work, Arp is gobbling up the disgusting parts. But I try not to think about that. While the fish cooks, I draw a picture of it. It makes me sad to draw it in the fire, though, so I draw it swimming up to fish heaven.

I'm so busy drawing that I don't notice how the fire is eating up our dinner until flames shoot into the sky. That isn't supposed to be part of the cycle of life! I quickly find a really long stick to poke our dinner out of the fire. The fish is totally black, but we don't care. It tastes delicious. We eat every bit we can. Arp has a nice long drink from the river. I wish I could drink that water too, but I just

take a few sips from my bottle. I don't have much water left. Then we fall asleep on our blanket even though the sun hasn't set yet.

I wake up when there's a light in my eyes. At first I think, Oh no! We've been rescued. But it isn't the State Patrol with a flashlight. The moon has risen above the trees and is shining down on us. I check my watch. It's only three in the morning. But I don't feel tired. In fact, I feel kind of excited. "Today's going to be the day!"

Arp doesn't say anything. He's probably thinking, How can today be the day when it isn't day yet?

But I pet him until he wakes up. I pack our stuff and put out what's left of the fire. Then we retrace our steps back along the stream. Going up is harder, but at least we aren't starving anymore. My main worry is that we won't be able to find the Trail in the dark. I don't want to walk in the stream and get my shoes wet. I'm sort of crashing through the bushes when I hear a strange sound like an animal growling. I don't think chipmunks and rabbits growl. I'm very worried that it's another bear. Then I realize the growling is actually snoring. And then I see a splotch of orange hanging on a tree limb. It's Trail Blaze Betty's hat!

I can't believe Trail Blaze Betty has followed us all the way to Massachusetts. It's very weird to find her right at the spot where we left the Trail, just like she was the other time when we went to the lake. It's like she's waiting for us to come back. I'm certainly not going to wake her up to ask her why. I pick up Arp and tiptoe around her as quietly as I can and get back on the smooth, wide Trail.

I like walking at night. Even though the moon is bright, I've never seen so many stars. In New York, you only see about three, and sometimes what you think is a star is a jet. But now there are millions above my head. I know those stars didn't just show up tonight; they're up there all the time. That makes me wonder how many other things are out there that most of the time you just can't see.

It's kind of like being friends with somebody. Your friend is still your friend even when you're not with her. If she is a real friend, I mean, and not a Patricia Palombo, who would forget all about you the moment you stopped admiring her outfits.

After about an hour, we start going uphill. And that

uphill is so UP that it has to be Mount Greylock. I m̶

how many mountains could there be in Massachusett

"I told you, Arp. Today's the day."

The sky gets lighter. I walk faster. Even though we ate that fish, I'm hungry again. I can't wait to get to the top of Mount Greylock. I wonder what else the store will sell. It has to have something besides postcards and Double Stuf Oreos. I can almost see the assortment of snacks. All those shiny colors I haven't seen in days, like bright red and orange and blue. All those different kinds of potato chips. Except I don't want snacks or even ice cream. I want a bucket of macaroni and cheese and a gallon of orange juice—without pulp. If they don't have dog food, I'll buy Arp a dozen Slim Jims. I should have enough money to get all that. I have ten whole dollars and four quarters—but those are for calling Lucy.

Yes, very soon, right after I eat the bucket of macaroni and drink the gallon of orange juice, I'll finally be able to call Lucy. I start practicing what I will say to her.

Hello, Lucy? This is Megan. I'm here at Mount Greylock.

Then I stop, because that's where SHE will say something. I try to imagine what that will be. Only I'm having trouble thinking of what she really WOULD say. All I can think of is what I want her to say.

Oh, Megan, I can't believe you made it. I'm so glad you're here!

Would she really say that? Or is she still mad at me

ot being a very good friend? But even if she is, she
n't stay mad at me after I tell her how sorry I am.

Arp sits down to scratch his ear and lick his paw.
Then he curls up in a ball to take a nap. Obviously he
has no idea what's waiting for us on top of this mountain.
So I have to carry him. But I'm not even mad about doing
this extra work, since we're so close to the end of our
long journey.

The sky turns pink as the sun rises. Now it doesn't
matter if anyone finds us. No one can send us home after
we make it! We're climbing higher and higher. The thick
green roof of leaves that has been over our heads gets
thinner and thinner. Any minute now, we'll be at the top
of Mount Greylock. My heart is pounding—well, I am
climbing pretty fast. But mostly I'm so excited that I
practically run the last few yards.

And there I am. Standing at the top. I'm the tallest
thing for miles and miles. I'm surrounded by rose-
colored sky in all directions. Slowly I turn in a complete
circle to admire the view.

Where's the tall gray stone monument? Where's the
store? Where's the food? More importantly, where's the
drinking fountain?

Nowhere. That's where.

17
Not Done Yet

I walk over and look behind a big pile of rocks. Like everything might be hiding there. But it isn't.

I sit down. *Plop.* Right where I am. I don't take one more step. I feel so totally defeated, I don't know what to do.

What happened?

Did I get on the wrong trail after we ate the fish? Did I go in the wrong direction? Did someone put blue splotches on the wrong trees just to trick me? Maybe that kid lied and I'm not even in Massachusetts. Maybe those horrible hikers lied and Mount Greylock isn't even on the Appalachian Trail. I can't believe it! All that work and all that suffering are wasted. I put my head down on my arms. But I can't even cry. I'm too exhausted.

On the day before the day before we were leaving for Vermont, I called Lucy to tell her a long list of things to bring. Her turquoise hoodie, because it gets cold up there at night. The *Calvin and Hobbes* collection of cartoons she promised to let me borrow. And thirty-six other things that I won't even bother to mention, because before I even got to the THIRD thing on the list, she said, "I can't come."

At first I thought she meant something else. "You mean not until the second week?"

But Lucy said, "No, I can't come."

So I said, "What? Are you grounded or something?" Which was a JOKE, because Lucy would never do anything bad to get grounded even before her mom got sick.

"Mom's sick again."

"But she had all the treatments. She's got to be better."

"The chemo didn't work."

"It made her hair fall out."

"It didn't get rid of all the cancer. They have to try something else. They're giving her a different kind of treatment."

But I didn't even ask what kind it was. I only cared about one thing. So I said, "When she's had the treatment, then can you come?"

"I don't know. I JUST CAN'T COME. Okay?" She sounded mad.

I didn't know why she should be mad at ME. I thought she should be mad at the doctors who didn't do a good enough job curing her mom. Since I couldn't say that, I said something really whiny. "But you promised."

"I never promised you, Megan."

"Yes you did."

For a moment it seemed like we were going to have one of those totally stupid arguments. You know the kind, where kids say "Yes you did" and "No I didn't" over and over until the world comes to an end. But we stopped.

We didn't say anything for a while. I would have thought she had hung up except that I heard her breathing. I heard me breathing too. I know I was waiting for her to say SOMETHING. Like maybe she was sorry? But she didn't. She was probably waiting for me to say that I was sorry. But I didn't. I said, "Fine then." I hung up really fast, because I could feel the crying creeping up the back of my throat and around the edges of my eyes.

The crying is creeping up around my eyes again. I thought I was done with crying and hearing that yucky voice in my head. But maybe I'm not—I mean, I also thought I was hiking to Mount Greylock.

I hear some people come huffing and puffing up the Trail. I don't bother to go to a better hiding place. What's the point? My trip is over anyway.

"What a view," a man says.

"Gorgeous," a woman says. "Look at those colors. I could try for a hundred years and never get them on paper."

"I just love it up here at this time of day," the man says.

"Me too," the woman says. "Shall we have our breakfast? I'm starving after that climb. Oh, hello. Who are you?"

Arp barks.

"What a cute little dog," the woman says.

"Where's your owner?" the man says. "Are you hungry? We don't have any dog food."

Arp barks again to beg for food. He's totally shameless. But I'm not going to stop him. I'm not going to do anything anymore ever again.

"Hey!" the man says.

Arp trots over behind the rocks with half a bagel in his mouth. He lies down right next to me to eat it. I would scold him, but what's the point? I mean, it's not like the people would want it back.

The man and woman come over and look at me. They stare for such a long time that I finally mumble, "Sorry."

"That's okay," the woman says. "I need to go on a diet anyway."

It's true; she is a little round. I consider offering to help her with her diet by eating the half she's holding in her hand. But I'm too upset to eat.

They're still staring at me. I look down at myself. My shoes are dirty and worn, like they walked thirty thousand miles. My legs are scratched, like they battled with a billion bushes. My calves have huge bulging muscles, like they hauled me up and down a thousand hills. My fingernails are black from building fires. My arms are brown from being outdoors for five days.

They look at each other. They look at Arp. Then they look at me again.

"Are you Megan?" the man says.

I shrug.

"How did you get here?" the woman says.

"We walked," I say.

"All the way from Vermont?" he says.

"It's all I can do to make it up this mountain," she says.

I shrug again.

"You must be starving." She goes over to their back-pack and takes out a bag of food. "Oh, isn't that cute?"

I turn around. Arp is sitting up and waving his paws. I didn't know he could do tricks like that.

"You little beggar," she says. "Did you really walk all that way too?"

She smiles as she gives Arp another bagel. Then she holds one out for me.

"Please take it. You need to eat something."

I eat it. But even if it were a New York bagel, it would still taste like sawdust.

"Can I have some water?" I say.

"Of course." The man gives me the bottle. I drink and drink until I can't drink anymore. Luckily it's a very big bottle. Then I put the cap back on and give it back to him.

"Thanks," I say.

"You're welcome," she says.

"Now we better get you home to your parents," he says.

"They must be frantic," she says.

"Please, not yet." Even though my journey is over, I still don't want it to end. I get up and walk toward the edge of the mountain. I look south. Toward Lucy? Who knows? Who cares? I messed up again.

The man comes over and stands next to me. "You see it?"

I shake my head. All I see is failure.

He points. I have no idea what I'm supposed to be looking at. It could be anything—a bird, a plane, a UFO. But in the distance, I see another mountain. And on top of it, a skinny stick glows in the early-morning light.

"What's that?" I say.

"Mount Greylock," he says.

THAT'S Mount Greylock? I stagger backward. I almost fall off the top of whatever the heck I'm standing on. "So what's this?"

"Mount Fitch," she says.

Mount Fitch? Can you believe I climbed the wrong mountain? And, besides that, it has such a dumb name. I mean, give me a break. Who would call a mountain Fitch?

It's so horrible that I have to laugh. I'm so many miles from that bucket of macaroni and cheese and that gallon of orange juice—and Lucy. I fall over laughing, in fact. I laugh until I'm crying again and Arp comes to see what's going on.

"What's so funny?" the woman says.

"Mount Fitch!" I say.

Then they laugh too. And Arp barks.

"Actually we like Mount Fitch better than Mount Greylock," she says.

"Mount Greylock is so crowded," he says.

"So many tourists just drive up there," she says.

"They aren't real hikers," he says.

"Like you," she says.

From the way she smiles, I know I have a chance. And then, when I notice a sketch pad in her backpack, I think I know how to persuade them to let me keep going.

"Are you an artist?" I ask her.

"Well, not much of one," she says.

"Sure you are. All you need is confidence," he says.

"Can I see?" I say.

The woman shows me her drawings. She has a hundred sketches of the same old tree. I guess all artists keep doing the same thing over and over, like my dad and his stone wall, and my mom and her barn.

Only as I study the woman's drawings, I see that it isn't just the same tree over and over. There are small changes. Things you might not think matter, but actually do. Like should the tree be from this angle or that, should it be in shadow or bright blazing sun, should the branch be a little bit longer or shorter?

"I like that drawing best," I say.

"You do? Why?" she says.

"Because in that one, the tree doesn't push you away; it brings you into the picture," I say.

"Look, Adam. She's right," she says.

"My parents are artists too," I say.

"Really?" she says.

"Just like you. Day after day, they work really hard to capture a heroic essence. Day after day, just like me going step after step on this long Trail," I say.

"Why are you?" he says.

"I have to get to Mount Greylock," I say.

"But why?" she says.

"It's something I have to do. It's my Hodgkin's Hike," I say.

"What kind of hike?" he says.

"The kind where you keep going no matter what," I say.

"People are very worried about you," she says.

"I know. I didn't plan that part. And I'm sorry. But it's just like how you have to keep drawing that same tree. I always used to quit. My parents always tried to teach me not to be like that. Only they couldn't. I had to do this hike to learn that the only way to fail is to quit."

"That's what you always tell me," she says to the man.

"I know," he says.

I stare at them. I'm not going to be a beggar like Arp. I'm just going to stand there calmly and confidently until they let me climb Mount Greylock.

"She's so close," she says.

"But her parents," he says.

"I think they'll understand," she says.

"I don't know," he says. "I hate to be responsible."

"And I hate to keep her from finishing her trip. She's come so far. I mean, look at her," she says.

He looks toward Mount Greylock. Then he looks at me.

"We'll be watching the news. If you haven't made it by tonight, we'll come looking for you," he says.

"Don't worry. I'll make it," I say.

They give me all their food and their water. The woman hugs me, and then she shakes my hand like I'm an important person.

Arp and I walk toward a blue splotch on the far side of Mount Fitch. As we start going down, I turn back to wave. "I really like that drawing," I call to her.

She smiles so happily that I don't tell her the real reason I like it. Her tree looks like the Hundred-Year-Old Maple.

18
Mount Greylock

The Trail is a huge long thing. It stretches all the way from Maine to Georgia. That's practically all of America, if you're going from top to bottom. (Well, duh, I guess that's why they made it like that.) Anyway, that huge long thing is so much bigger than you are, and bigger than anything you can imagine, that at first hiking it seems impossible. But when you're actually walking on it, you realize that this whole huge thing is just step after step after step, oops don't trip on that root, hmm wonder what that ugly plant is called, ouch that bug bit me. Step after step, some up, some down, some easy, some hard. And that's how you get it done. One little bit at a time.

The end is in sight.

Well, actually the end WAS in sight when I was standing on top of Mount Fitch and feeling powerful and wise. But as soon as I go back on the Trail and climb down Mount Fitch, Mount Greylock gets hidden by the leaves. Going down seems like such a total waste of energy because obviously we're only going to have to climb BACK UP again. And while I'm on the subject of climbing up and down a million hills, the next time somebody makes a long trail that stretches all across the United States, maybe they could put it in a FLAT place!

And oh, by the way, it starts to rain.

At first it's just a few drops. Just a few wet splotches landing *plop* on my hat.

"Maybe whoever is in charge of the weather will take pity on us since we're so close," I say to Arp.

But obviously nobody is in charge of the weather, because then it really starts pouring. Oh great. Now what are we going to do?

I start to run. But then I stop. Where do I think I'm running to? I mean, it's not like I can go inside. I have a choice of trees to stand under. That's all.

I'm desperate enough to get out the rain poncho. By that point, I don't care if I look like a nerd. But even after I put it over Arp and me, the rain leaks through. I'm getting more and more miserable. And don't you dare say, Well, at least the rain chased away the mosquitoes. Or, You shouldn't complain; you've been really lucky with the weather so far. Or, What do you expect? Do you think you're hiking through a desert? And please do NOT be like my dad and give me a whole long lecture that ends with the saying "Into each life some rain must fall."

There isn't anything to do except keep going.

Actually there is one good thing about the rain. We're the only ones crazy enough to be out hiking in it.

Of course, I have to carry Arp. I can't even bribe him with the rest of those bagels because there's no way to tell when we're going to get to the store on top of Mount Greylock. I can't see it anymore. Huge clouds are sitting on top of the mountain. Meanwhile, the rain is turning the Trail into a river of mud.

My hike is falling apart. In fact, I'm starting to fall apart too. I mean, it was bad enough being tired and hungry. But now I'm wet and muddy AND tired and hungry. Instead of doing the last few miles in total awesome triumph, I'm sloshing along. I can't even think about how close I am to Lucy. Or whether she'll be glad to see me. All I can think is, I've got to make it up this last mountain.

After we share a soggy bagel for our lunch, the Trail starts going up again.

"This is it, Arp. This is Mount Greylock. For real this time." I put him down. "This is the end of our journey. You have to do it on your own four feet."

The rain has mostly ended, but we still get showers when drops fall off the leaves. We pass under trees that tower over us like wise old giants. Everything feels solemn, except the birds are really chattering away. Maybe they're just glad the storm has ended and they can eat the lovely mosquitoes that will soon be swarming around again. But it seems like the birds are saying to me, "You did it!"

And you know what? I did do it. The girl who thought she couldn't do anything, who always quit, who hated the Woods—that girl hiked all the way from Vermont to Massachusetts, with just her little dog and not nearly enough food and all kinds of worries. But she didn't let anything stop her. No matter how dark it got or how lonely and hungry she got, she kept going.

And somehow or other I SURVIVED!

When Arp and I come out of the Woods, we're on top of Mount Greylock. But we don't rush right over to find the store. I think we better scope out the situation. So I feed Arp the last bagel while we hide in the bushes at the edge of a carpet of grass. Yes, real grass that somebody actually cut with a lawn mower. In the center of the grass is a tall tower made of gray stone. Its sides curve in as it rises into the sky. On its top is a huge sphere that looks like it could send signals to outer space. I feel like they built that huge monument just for me.

The sun is setting. But this time I'm not worried about the dark that's coming. This time the color is just part of the celebration.

I'm here. I'm finally really and truly here.

You'll never believe what happens next. A car drives by.

Excuse me? A CAR? On a ROAD?

I know people do drive up here. How else could they have a store? Besides, I can see a few other cars in a parking lot that's way off to the right side of the grass. But still, it doesn't seem right that someone just drives up in a car after I nearly KILLED myself hiking to get here.

That person turns out to be a Park Ranger, which makes me nervous, since Rangers are like policemen. I very quietly pick up Arp and slip deeper into the bushes.

The car stops near a family that's sitting on the grass in little camp chairs. The Ranger leans out the window and says, "The park closes an hour after sunset."

The park closes? I have to cover my mouth so I won't burst out laughing. Give me a break. How can they close the park? What are they going to do? Put away all the trees? Roll up the carpet of grass? Will the animals take off their fur suits and go home?

The mom says, "We better start packing up then. Go buy your ice cream."

The kids run over to a cute little stone house next to the parking lot. That must be the souvenir store. They tug at the door, but it won't open. So they run back.

"It closed at six, Mom!" one of the kids says.

"Oh, well. Get in the car. We'll stop someplace else on the way home."

Can you believe it? After all those days and nights of hiking, I'm too late! I would be really upset, except that my stomach is way too nervous for eating anyway. I take a big drink of water from the bottle the tree-artist woman gave me. Then I stare at the stone house. On the wall is a pay phone. Luckily it's outside, so I can still call Lucy.

I check my watch. It's eight-fifteen.

I know that Lucy, Alison, and Mrs. T. are done watching TV. This summer they all watched this one show Alison liked. They had a whole ritual for watching it. First Lucy brought big pillows so they could all sit up in Alison's bed. Then Mrs. T. brought the snacks, because she's like me. TV commercials make her feel starving, since they're always about food and they always show the food in particularly yummy ways—you know, with the cheese all melty and the chocolate chunks really huge. Of course, the snacks would not be pizza or chocolate chip cookies. The snacks would probably be fruit and other healthy things. Even though Lucy wasn't not-eating anymore, she insisted on eating things that are good for you. As you know by now, Lucy is like that. She always does what's right. Anyway, Lucy, Alison, and Mrs. T. all snuggled together and watched *Jeopardy*.

Now I had never heard of the TV show *Jeopardy*. I didn't even have a clue what the word meant, so I asked Dad. He told me to find it in the dictionary because looking up words is a skill I'm supposed to learn. But I couldn't find the word, because I was spelling it wrong. (Maybe you can tell me what's the point of putting that *o* in there.) So Mom helped me.

Jeopardy means DANGER. EXPOSURE TO IMMINENCE OF DEATH.

That sounded like a TERRIBLE show for Alison to watch. Unless, I thought, it had a superhero character who always showed up at the end of the episode to save somebody from whatever jeopardy he was in that day— snakes or hurricanes or mutant mosquitoes from outer space.

Now you're probably laughing, because of course you know what the show is. You've seen it, right? Well, before you think I'm a total idiot, let me remind you that I'm NOT allowed to watch unlimited amounts of TV. Even when I wasn't being punished for almost killing the Hundred-Year-Old Maple, I only got one hour of screen time each day. And believe me, I wasn't about to waste that hour flipping around to shows I didn't already know were really good.

But after Lucy told me about it, I decided to watch it too. Doing what she was doing would be almost like spending time with her.

Imagine my shock when there weren't any giant spiders or tsunamis. No heroes with muscular bodies. No superpowers or clever gadgets. Just a doofus in a suit and three other doofuses trying to answer questions. Boy, was I mad about wasting thirty minutes on that! But I watched the whole half hour just in case the good part was coming. It wasn't.

When I called Lucy on Saturday, I asked her how she could stand to watch a boring quiz show. She said her mom liked it because there were ANSWERS. Yes, actual answers were written in those little boxes. And what's more, the little boxes were organized by categories, so you always knew what you were getting.

Every night, Lucy, Alison, and Mrs. T. wrote down their answers to the final question. Then the TV played that music. When the music was over, you found out immediately if you were right or wrong. Nobody had to wait for test results, which Lucy said always drove her mom crazy. Boy, did I know how she felt. Kind of, I mean. Because I was only finding out what grade I got in math. But the tests she was finding out about really were for life or death. Had the new treatment worked? Had her cancer finally gone away this time? Or was it still there?

Now I remember that the last time I spoke to Lucy, on the day I fell out of the tree, they were waiting to hear from the doctor. They were waiting for the final Jeopardy answer.

My stomach is churning so much that I have to sit down in the bushes and hide my head in my hands. How could I have been such a bad friend to Lucy? It was so selfish to want her with me. It must have seemed like I hardly cared about Alison at all.

And like I hardly cared about my own mom. Or my dad. Or even my sister.

Arp comes over and licks my hands. Maybe he's being nice, or maybe there's cream cheese on my fingers. I pick him up and hug him much tighter than he likes. But he lets me. So maybe it isn't just because of the cream cheese.

I pull myself up and carry Arp over to the pay phone. After I set him down in some pink petunias that are planted along the building, I put two of the quarters in the slot and punch the buttons. I hear just a short ring. Then someone answers in a big hurry, like she's been sitting right by the phone, waiting and waiting for someone to call, hoping and hoping for good news. Hoping that it will be life, and not death.

"Hello?"

"Mom?"

"Oh, Megan, thank God," Mom says.

Then I'm crying and Mom is crying and calling to Dad and Ginia. I hear them shouting in the background. We're all so happy—even Arp, who's gobbling up a hot dog he found in the petunias.

19
Journey's End

I hang up the phone. I let out a huge sigh of relief. My family will be here in about an hour. That seems so strange. I mean, it took me five days and four nights to get to the top of Mount Greylock. Actually it took my whole life to get to this place.

Only I can't celebrate yet. I still have to make another phone call. I want to call Lucy more than anything. But I'm nervous too. I've been gone for so long. What if Alison got sicker? I sigh again. That would be awful. But there's only one way to find out and that's to call.

Unfortunately, just when I'm going to put in my last two quarters, I hear a car. Doesn't that Ranger have anything better to do than waste gas by making loops around an empty park? It probably won't matter if he finds me now, but I pick up Arp and slip back into the Woods.

It's getting dark. But darkness doesn't bother me

anymore. I can still see the stone tower, since it's a lighter gray than the sky. While I'm waiting, I draw a picture of it, with me standing on top, of course. Then I add Lucy.

Arp barks.

"Be quiet. I'm going to put you in the picture," I whisper. Before I can figure out where to squeeze him in, he runs off into the Woods.

"Arp!" I hiss. I can't believe he's gone after another rabbit. Hasn't he learned by now he's never going to catch one? I almost hope that he finally does; this is the last chance he'll get.

After a little while he trots back to me. His tail is wagging, like he's really proud of himself. Only he doesn't have a rabbit. He's bringing Trail Blaze Betty! It's too dark to see her face, but I recognize her bent legs and her orange hat.

I'm stunned. How could Arp do this to me?

I get to my feet, but it's too late to run anywhere. All I can do is apologize. "Look, I know I lied about my parents being with me on the Trail. I don't have eight people in my family, so I shouldn't have taken eight brownies. I shouldn't have eaten them all at once either. I'm sorry. I'll pay you back for them. I have ten dollars."

Trail Blaze Betty holds out her hand. At first, I think she wants the money. But instead, she grabs my hand and shakes it.

"You did it, Girl. Had my doubts sometimes. But you did it."

Arp is jumping up against her legs until she bends down to scratch behind his ears. "You too, little fellow. You hiked the whole way."

I'm going to point out that actually I carried him for a lot of those miles. But I don't want to spoil the moment.

"You set a tough pace this last stretch. Mind if I sit down?" she says.

"Oh no." I sit down too.

She slips off her pack and then lowers herself to the ground. She grunts when she plops the last few inches. She takes a water bottle and a package out of her pack. She opens the package and takes out a thin brown strip. She offers it to me. "Go on. It's pemmican."

I am suspicious because of my recent tofu experience. But I take a nibble. It's hard to chew, but it's not too bad. "Thanks. What did you say it was?"

"Dried buffalo."

I nearly choke. "Are you serious?"

"Native Americans eat it. I left in such a hurry I couldn't get any decent food ready. Had to just take whatever dried food I had. Here. Have some water."

She offers me the bottle. I take a drink. Then I give her back the bottle. "So why did you leave in such a hurry? Did you follow me because you were mad?"

"Angry? No. Crazy maybe."

"Crazy?"

"To let you do this. But if I was going to let you, I figured I better keep an eye on you. Got really mad when you left the Trail those two times. Thought for sure you'd get lost. But you found your way back."

"Thank you for letting me."

"I only let you because it seemed important for you to do it."

"It was."

I'm afraid she'll want me to say how or why or something. But luckily she isn't the kind of grown-up who thinks it's necessary to TALK about stuff after you've already done it. She scratches Arp's ears. Then she says, "I had a selfish reason too."

I remember what she said when I met her. "You want more kids to hike?"

"That's right."

"Well, more kids should!"

"But not on their own." She points a stick of dried buffalo at me.

"Oh no. I wouldn't go alone again." It'd be much more fun to hike with Lucy. We could even start a club at school and get lots of kids to go. I bet if Patricia Palombo went hiking, she might actually become a girl you could like.

"The next time there's an Appalachian Trail meeting and the old people are worried that kids hate hiking, Arp and I will come and prove that we don't. Right, Arp?"

Arp is napping. He opens one eye when he hears his name. He doesn't seem excited. But he will be. I know that when we get back to New York City, he'll miss the days when he could run after rabbits whenever he wanted.

Trail Blaze Betty gives Arp a pat. "We'd be honored to have you both at our next meeting. Oh! I almost forgot!" She digs around in her pack. I'm hoping she has more brownies. But she pulls out a book and hands it to me. It's my copy of My Side of the Mountain.

"I found it by one of your campsites. Figured you left it behind by mistake."

The mistake was not throwing it further! But I'm glad to have the book back. I flip past a few pages. I see sketches of plants I could have eaten and a drawing of how to carve a fishhook. I stick the book in my backpack. My trip didn't turn out so bad without it. But when I go with my hiking club, I'll bring the book so we'll know what to do.

Then a light shines on me like I'm doing something I shouldn't.

"Is that you? Megan Knotts?"

It's the Ranger. I know my trip is over and my family is on its way, but I still don't like being caught. I scrunch down and turn my face away from the light. Then the light shines on Trail Blaze Betty.

"Are you all right? Who's that with you?"

The Ranger sounds suspicious, so I stand up to explain. "It's Trail Blaze Betty. She looks after the Appalachian Trail."

"Come on out of there," the Ranger says.

I can't see him very well because the light is still shining in my face, but he sounds mad. "It's okay. I called my parents. We're just waiting for them."

"Your parents contacted the State Patrol, and they contacted me. You need to wait for them in my car."

I don't want to wait in a car. I want to enjoy my last moments in the Woods. "Oh no, we're fine here. Thanks just the same."

"I want you in the car. Right now. Before anything else happens."

I'm getting a very bad feeling. But I can't argue with the Ranger. I pick up my backpack. I call to Arp. I push out through the bushes. Trail Blaze Betty comes too. The Ranger opens the car door.

"Want me to wait with you?" Trail Blaze Betty shifts from foot to foot.

I can see that she's really uncomfortable. I don't like the way the Ranger is staring at her. I'm afraid she'll get in trouble. And I don't want that to happen. "It's okay. You better find someplace to camp."

"Don't worry about me. I can bunk down in the shelter over there."

She points to another stone building behind the store.

"That's a shelter?" I say. It looks a million times better than the one she built.

She grins like she knows what I'm thinking. "You bet. But it fills up fast, so if you're all right, I better make sure they've got space for me."

"I'm fine," I say.

"Good-bye, then. Good job. See you at that meeting!" She pats Arp.

I'm wondering, Do hikers hug? Or do they just sort of bump backpacks?

"Thank you. For everything," I say.

She shakes my hand again. I watch her walk away until her crazy orange hat and her bent legs disappear around the side of the building.

I kind of wish I could go with her. The Ranger is making me nervous. And then I hear sirens wailing in the distance.

"What's that all about?" I say. But I know. They're coming for me.

"You had a whole lot of people worrying about you," the Ranger says.

"I know. I'm sorry."

The sirens get louder and closer. Arp barks as a whole parade of vehicles swoop up the road. Now I really want to run away. But I can't. I have to face what I've done.

There are two police cars, an ambulance, and a news van. At first I think, WOW! I'm going to be on TV! Now Patricia Palombo can't brag about the time the back of her head was on the six o'clock news when she was a snowflake in the Macy's Thanksgiving Day Parade.

I take off my hat. Then I put it back on and pull it down over my eyes. Maybe the hat looks dumb, but my hair must look a whole lot worse. Besides, I don't want to explain why I did it to anybody but Lucy. So I pick up Arp and get in the Ranger's car.

The Ranger stays outside.

The cars stop. Even brighter lights practically blind me. People run toward the Ranger's car, shouting. "Megan, where were you? How did you get here from Vermont? Are you all right, Megan?"

Lights flash as people take my picture in the car. Somebody wheels out a stretcher. I start to laugh about it, except it reminds me of how worried everybody must have been.

Arp is barking like crazy, so I can hardly hear what the Ranger is saying. But eventually the Ranger and the police get the reporters to line up to wait for my family.

I get out the book. Holding it makes me feel a little less nervous.

Finally I see my family's car drive up. It stops on the far side of the grass. Mom gets out. She stands there, peering at all the other cars, searching for me in the spinning red lights. The camera lights blaze on her face. She looks so worried, not being able to see me.

I get out of the Ranger's car. I'm going to run to her. But suddenly, after all that hiking, my legs don't want to work anymore.

It doesn't matter. She runs to me and grabs on to me like she's never going to let me go. Dad and Ginia are right behind her. The reporters start to close in, but the police keep them back.

We're all hugging and crying. Now I don't have to worry anymore about my tears wasting water. Arp barks and jumps against my legs. I pick him up so he won't feel so short and left out. But he keeps barking. I'm glad he's talking, because I don't know what to say. Hiking the Trail seems so much easier than watching my mom cry.

"I'm so sorry. I know you were worried. I left you notes. Did that girl send the e-mail?"

Mom nods.

"You could have called. Why didn't you call?" Dad's voice cracks. He's actually shaking he's so upset.

"But I couldn't call." I'm about to make a dumb excuse like, You didn't give me a cell phone. That's what the old Megan would say. Now that I've stopped hiking and I'm with my family again, maybe the old Megan will come back. And maybe the yucky voice will come back too.

Mom reaches over to take Arp from me. She holds him on his back in her arms like he's her baby again. Only he's not; he's my Loyal Dog. So I take Arp out of her arms and put him on the ground. Then I stand up straighter, like I'm on top of the monument, and I say, "I couldn't call because you would have stopped me from hiking. And I had to do something. On my own. Like you're always telling me to."

"We never told you to run away," Dad says.

So I give him the book. Then he frowns and looks at Mom, who shakes her head.

"I know it was terrible to make you worry. I know you're probably going to ground me. But Arp and I did an amazing thing."

Then they all look at me like they're seeing me for the first time. Which is really kind of true, because they haven't ever seen this Megan before.

"Yes, you did an amazing thing," Dad says.

"But you *are* going to be grounded," Mom says.

I nod. Actually I'm so exhausted that I won't mind staying home for a while.

"And you'll have to make reparations to all those people who spent all that time searching for you," Dad says.

I sigh just thinking of all the poems I'll have to write.

Oh, search parties, dear search parties,
Thanks for all that spying.
Even though you never found me,
I appreciate your trying.

"And help us pay them back. Helicopters cost a lot, you know," Mom says.

I swallow. I'm afraid to ask how much. Since I don't get that big of an allowance, I could be in debt for the rest of my life.

Then Ginia says, "I'll help pay."

"You will?" I can't believe it. Ginia NEVER loans me money, not even for just ten minutes when we're at the

227

corner deli and I forgot to bring a dollar for ice cream.

Then she starts crying. "It's my fault that you got lost. I never should have said those things about Lucy. I never should have let you out of my sight. I should have looked for you right away. But I wanted to be with Sam. So I convinced myself you had gone back and left with Mom and Dad."

I wish the cameras were rolling, because Ginia has never apologized to me before in her whole life. Then I'm glad they're not; her eyes are so red and puffy that she looks pretty awful.

"It's okay." I can't be mad at her when everything turned out great.

Ginia hugs me and I hug her. For the first time in practically forever, I'm glad I have a sister.

Dad goes to talk to the police. Then the reporters surround us. Cameras flash. Microphones hover over our heads. "Just a few questions. Megan, are you all right?"

"I feel great," I say.

"Did you really walk here all the way from Vermont?" a reporter says.

"Yes," I say. Then I think of Trail Blaze Betty and how I can get in a commercial for the Appalachian Trail. "Actually, no."

"You got a ride?" a reporter says.

"Did you hitchhike?" another reporter says.

"Then you were kidnapped?" another reporter says.

"No! I didn't walk. I hiked! Hiking is a great thing to do. Anybody can do it. Old people, young people, little dogs, everybody should hike the Appalachian Trail!"

"Everybody should hike with their parents," Mom says.

"With their parents," I say.

"Mrs. Knotts, you must be so glad to have your daughter back."

"I am. But Megan is really exhausted. We need to get her home so she can have a nice bath and a good night's sleep."

Mom hasn't changed one bit. She and Ginia walk over to Dad and the car. But I don't follow them. I stand there and Arp stays with me.

"What's wrong, Megan?" Mom says.

"I want to finish my trip," I say.

"Were you going all the way to Georgia?" Ginia says.

"I was going to see Lucy."

"Lucy? Who's Lucy?" the reporters buzz.

I don't answer. I can't call her my best friend until she forgives me.

"It's so late, Megan. I really think it would be better if you wait," Mom says.

"I can't wait. I came all this way for her. I climbed this mountain for her and her mom."

"For Alison?"

"To show her that you have to keep trying. Even if you get sick again and the news is bad and it starts to rain, you have to keep trying."

I know I'm not making any sense. But I keep talking because I can't believe Mom is still walking to the car. Isn't she listening at all?

"Mom, why can't we go tonight?" Ginia says.

But Mom doesn't listen to her either. She gets in the car.

I talk louder so she can hear me. Now I'm almost shouting. "The only way to fail is to quit and you never ever want me to quit, do you?"

Then Mom gets out of the car and hands me the shiny silver cell phone. "You better call Lucy and tell her that you're coming over. We should have called her before. She's been so worried about you too."

I hug Mom. Then we all get in the car. I give Mom back the phone so she can call. I'm too full of feelings to talk. After Mrs. T. finishes shouting for joy, Mom gets directions. It isn't very far. We drive down the winding mountain road in silence. I can tell my family has a thousand questions. But I'm grateful they save them for later.

Dad turns onto a long, curving driveway. I ask him to stop so Arp and I can walk up that last little hill.

The house is dark except for one light outside and a blue TV light in a downstairs window. Lucy is waiting for us on the front porch.

When she sees us, she comes running. But before she

can put her arms around me, I say, "Wait! I want you to know I'm sorry that I got mad at you for wanting to practice saving people and I'm sorry I ate the egg-salad sandwich."

"It's okay, Megan." Lucy tries to hug me again. But I hold up my hand.

"Let me finish. Please? Okay. I'm sorry that I wasn't more understanding when you couldn't come to Vermont and I'm sorry that I complained about my slimy hair when you were waiting for the doctor to call."

"Can I hug you now?"

I think for a minute. I'm probably forgetting something. But I don't want to keep saying sorry forever, so I just say, "I'm sorry I wasn't a better friend when you were worrying about your mom. Do you forgive me?"

"Oh, Megan."

Then she hugs me. I hear a sniffing sound. Is she crying? Or is she trying not to smell me? "I did go swimming. Once. But I probably really stink."

"I bet it kept the bugs away."

Good old Lucy, always looking on the bright side.

"How's your mom?" I say.

"Okay," Lucy says.

But she always said that, even when Alison wasn't. So I say, "I mean really. What did the doctor say?"

"It's good news. So far, they haven't found any more bad spots."

"That's great!" I say.

Lucy nods. "We're keeping our fingers crossed."

I'm so happy I hug Lucy again.

Then Mrs. T. comes out onto the porch and joins our hug. "Here's our hero. Our inspiration!"

"You know, when your mom called after they found your note, and they said you were hiking, we couldn't believe it. I mean, no offense, Megan, but . . . ," Lucy says.

"I know, I know. I never used to want to walk anywhere," I say.

"If the theater was more than two blocks from the restaurant, you always wanted to take a taxi," Mrs. T. says.

"I know, I know," I say.

"But look at you now," Mrs. T. says.

I hope they aren't looking at me too closely. "It's a good thing it's dark because you would NOT believe my hair. I don't think I'll ever be able to comb it."

"You're a real Nature Girl," Lucy says.

We all laugh, but I can tell she's proud of me. And that makes me happy.

"Where's your family?" Mrs. T. says. "Don't they want to come in?"

"They're waiting down there in the car. It's so late, they thought Alison would be asleep."

"She is. But I'll go say hello to them. If you can hike up Mount Greylock, I guess I can manage this hill." Mrs. T. walks down the driveway.

"You're probably really tired," Lucy says.

"Yes. I am."

I know it's time for us to leave. Only I still have so much to tell Lucy. And I know I won't be allowed to call her. I wasn't even through being punished for almost killing the Hundred-Year-Old Maple. Who knows what kind of consequences I'll get for making everybody worry.

But I have to be brave about saying good-bye. "I'll write you, okay? I'll send you the pictures I drew on the Trail. Then, in September, we'll be back at school together—if we're not in different classes again. You can join my new hiking club—if you aren't in knitting club with Patricia Palombo. We can always see each other after school—if there isn't too much homework in seventh grade."

It's all sounding worse and worse.

Then Lucy says, "While you were gone, I got so worried about you. I was talking about it to this social worker who's always really nice to us, and not just because it's her job. Anyway, I told her how I was supposed to visit you, but I never felt like I could leave my mom for even a second. That if I did leave her, she would get sicker."

"You don't have to explain. I understand all that now. I shouldn't have been bugging you about it. I was wrong and selfish."

Lucy grabs my arm. "Let me tell you what the social worker said. She told me lots of kids feel responsible.

But they didn't make their parents get sick. How could they? They're just kids. And kids are supposed to have fun. My mom completely agreed. In fact, she'd been feeling guilty that her cancer was ruining my summer. And feeling guilty isn't good for her. She says the best way I can help her get better is to have fun."

"That's great!" I'm glad that Lucy can enjoy the rest of her summer. She actually looks like the good old Lucy. She's smiling and her head is tilted to one side, like it always does whenever she's thinking of a fabulous adventure. I get a little sad that we can't have it together.

"Well?" she says.

She's waiting. Only I don't know what I'm supposed to say. We stand there for a little while. Then I say, "Well, good-bye."

I hug her one last time and start down the driveway. I hear her run up the porch steps and then run back down the steps to catch up to me.

"Here, Nature Girl." She hands me her backpack.

"What's this?" I say.

"My pajamas, my toothbrush, my *Calvin and Hobbes* book, my turquoise hoodie, and four changes of clothes," she says.

Then I get it. I start jumping up and down. Arp gets excited and jumps too. "You mean you're coming with us right now?"

"Yes. If you're going in the car. I don't think I can hike all the way back to Vermont."

234

I hug Lucy. Together we each grab one strap of the backpack and run down the little hill to the car. We run so fast, the backpack sails up in the air. It's like we're flying up and around the tower on top of Mount Greylock. Like nothing can stop us, so long as we're together.

Dad and Mom and Ginia are all outside the car talking to Mrs. T. Lucy and I are running too fast to put on the brakes, so we crash into everybody.

"Mom! Dad! Can Lucy come? I know I'm grounded, but maybe she could be grounded with me? And our punishment can be hiking and no TV and extra *ART* time?"

Dad and Mom laugh. But then they get serious.

"I don't know," Dad says.

"You still need some consequences," Mom says.

Of course, not being with Lucy is the worst consequence of all. But there is something that would be almost as bad.

"What if . . ." I pause; I'm not sure I want to suggest this. "What if I only eat tofu the whole rest of the summer?"

"That's not a punishment," Mom says.

"Oh yes it is!" the rest of us say.

Mom shakes her head. "You better think of something else."

Then I tell them about my idea for starting a hiking club and keeping the Trail clean like Trail Blaze Betty does. Mom likes the sound of that.

So it's agreed. We say good-bye to Mrs. T. Dad puts Lucy's backpack in the trunk. Then we drive to Vermont, where the summer can begin all over again.

It feels strange to be riding in a car, back to Vermont. Only I'm not really undoing all the miles I hiked. In my mind, I'm still hiking. I'll always be hiking. No matter what else is going on in my life, no matter how much trash people dump on my Trail or how hard seventh grade is, I won't let anything bother me. I'll just keep remembering how my Loyal Dog and I hiked the Appalachian Trail. And survived!

Author's Note

The Appalachian Trail really does pass through Vermont and Massachusetts as it stretches from Georgia to Maine. However, Megan's journey and all the people she meets are fictional. To tell her story, I have invented many landmarks and left out others. But you can really climb Mount Greylock. If you make it to the top, you'll see the stone tower and you'll be able to buy a snack—unless the store has closed for the day!

jane Kelley lives in Brooklyn, New York, with her husband and daughter. She has enjoyed many summers in Vermont. This is her first book.